Mary's
Little
Donkey

and the
Escape to Egypt

Mary's Little Donkey

and the
Escape to Egypt

Gunhild Sehlin

Floris
Books

Translated by Hugh Latham and Donald Maclean
Illustrations by Jan Verheijn
Cover illustration by Hélène Muller

Originally published in Swedish under the title
Marias lilla åsna in 1962 and *Åsnan och barnet* in 1964
Mary's Little Donkey first published in English
in 1979 by Floris Books
Mary's Little Donkey and the Flight to Egypt
first published in English in 1987 by Floris Books
This third edition published 2012 by Floris Books
Third printing 2017

Copyright © 1962, 1964 Gunhild Sehlin and
Almqvist & Wiksell Förlag AB, Stockholm
This translation © Floris Books, 1979, 1987, 2012

British Library CIP data available
ISBN 978-086315-933-6
Printed in Poland

Contents

The laziest donkey in the whole of Nazareth

Long, long ago a little donkey lived in Nazareth, in the Holy Land. He was quite different from all the other donkeys in the town. He was as lazy and untidy and dirty as they were clean and hardworking. All the same, he moved very beautifully and he held his head the highest of them all.

Sometimes all the donkeys rambled along in a long line carrying firewood from the little wood right into Nazareth. They all trotted along eagerly. They always tried to see who could carry the most wood home to his master. Right at the end of the line, the lazy donkey shambled along and whenever he had the chance to shake off a few branches, that's just what he did. Sometimes he tried to push past one or two of his comrades, because he didn't like being last. But the others always kicked out at him and stopped him, saying, "Stay where you belong, you lazy donkey!"

In the evening when all the donkeys came home to their stalls, they were combed and brushed until their coats shone like silk. Now, the lazy donkey belonged to the richest man in Nazareth, but he had absolutely the laziest groom to look after him. The groom never combed him and that's why the donkey always ran around dirty and with matted hair. It annoyed the other donkeys that he held his head so proudly anyway.

"Aren't you ashamed?" they said, "Fancy stretching out your neck and strutting around when you're so dirty."

And the oldest and wisest donkey said, "Don't you understand? It just isn't right. You can't give yourself airs and look as dirty as you do."

But the lazy donkey was not at all worried. "I'll show them one day," he thought.

Of course he didn't really know what he was going to show them, only that it would be something wonderfully beautiful and strange.

The people of the little town often laughed at the lazy donkey. "He should watch it, or he'll starve one day," they said. "He's almost too lazy to eat."

Even his master sighed sometimes. "He looks really terrible. Simon, get on with it now and comb him thoroughly."

"Yes, master," answered Simon.

But as soon as his master had gone, Simon hung the brush on its nail and lay in the grass. And so sometimes the little donkey was only half combed. Then the people and the animals laughed and mocked him even more.

"Just wait!" the little donkey thought to himself, "I'll show you all, one day." But he didn't say anything.

From time to time, Simon had to fetch water from the town well. He didn't like doing this at all, because he thought it was work a woman should do, but he had to obey when his master gave the order. He threw two leather water buckets over the donkey's back and the pair set off. If the groom felt that they were going too slowly, he drove the donkey on with a stick. But that didn't happen very often, because Simon was lazy too and wasn't usually in a hurry.

Early in the morning it was always lively and busy at the well, because all the women were fetching water in large, earthenware jugs. They filled their jugs up to the brim with clear, fresh water and carried them home on their heads. The women were very skilful, and not one of them spilt a single drop of the precious water, and no one dropped a jug. Often the women sat for a little while by the well and chatted before returning home, but not for long, because they wanted to get back while the morning was still fresh and cool.

One morning a young woman, whose name was Mary, met Simon and his donkey. She was on the way home with her jug of water. Mary looked at the little donkey and said: "What a beautiful donkey! It's such a pity that he's so dirty."

She stopped for a minute and stroked the donkey behind his ears. How lovely that was! He couldn't remember ever having been stroked before. And on the way home he was thinking so much about Mary that he didn't notice when Simon shouted and hit and thumped him.

From that day on, the lazy donkey often saw Mary at the same time at the well. And every time she had a friendly word for the little animal, and she stroked him.

When the donkey went trotting along home after this, he held his head even higher than usual. All his comrades grumbled. They said: "What's the matter with him now? Every day he makes himself out to be more important, and at the same time he gets lazier and lazier. It's disgraceful!"

But the little donkey took no notice at all of what they said.

"If only they knew!" he thought to himself.

Every morning now the donkey pricked up his ears and tried to hear if Simon was being sent by his master to the well. If the groom came along with the water buckets he was so delighted and happy, he could hardly keep still while they were being fastened. Then he set off to the well so quickly, uphill and downhill, that the astonished Simon could scarcely keep up.

If Mary wasn't there, the donkey thought she must be late. Then he would wriggle and kick as soon as Simon wanted to fasten the water containers on, and so it would take longer before they were ready to set out for home. Even then he would plant his legs firm and refuse to budge, and get himself whipped and beaten, keeping it up until Mary came and stroked him and spoke some friendly words to him.

After that he trotted home happily, and held his head high.

"He is quite mad," Simon said to the other grooms when he came home.

***

One day, the donkey trod on a sharp piece of stone. After this every step he took was painful; it made him limp.

"That's his punishment," the other donkeys said. "It serves him right. Let's see him try to trot proudly now!"

Mary noticed it next morning. She asked, "What's wrong with the donkey's foot? Has he hurt himself?"

"I don't think so," Simon answered, who hadn't even noticed that the donkey was limping.

"It's a shame not to help the poor animal," Mary said angrily.

"There's nothing wrong with him," replied Simon. "He's just lazy and vicious."

"Can I just have a look at your foot?" Mary asked the donkey.

"Watch out, he'll kick," warned Simon. "It's dangerous to touch his hoofs."

"He'll let me," Mary said.

Willingly, the donkey lifted his foot and kept quite still. Mary found the sharp piece of stone and pulled it out.

"So that was the problem," Mary said. "Now you can go on trotting about so beautifully and upright."

When the donkey came home, his comrades were all angry because he could walk and run again. They grumbled a lot. But it didn't bother the lazy donkey one little bit.

"If only they knew!" he thought. "Oh, if only they knew!"

The sale of the donkey

With her jug of water on her head, Mary strolled home. She had to go a long way through the narrow, winding alleys. She was exhausted when at last she reached her house. She put the jug down, sat down on a bench in her garden, and rested.

Joseph, her husband, came out of his workshop. He always took great care of Mary, and when he saw how tired she was, he was worried.

"If only I could buy you a donkey," he sighed. "He could carry the water and firewood for you, and you wouldn't have to drag such heavy things about."

"That would be wonderful," said Mary. "I would love to have a donkey. But we both know that we can't afford to buy one. Don't worry, Joseph. When I've had a bit of rest, I can carry on. God gives me the strength. Just wait, you'll see."

So Joseph went back into his workshop. He had to work from dawn to dusk to make enough money to feed them both. That's why he was so sad that he didn't have enough money to buy a donkey.

As he stood there and planed the wood, an idea came to him. "If I got up an hour earlier every day, and worked faster, I might be able to earn enough extra money to pay for a donkey," he said to himself. "I must try. Mary looked so tired today."

From this day on, Joseph got up before it was light and worked as hard as he could. Fortunately he had enough orders. Slowly but surely, his savings grew bigger.

"Dear Joseph," Mary said many times, "you're working too hard. We have money for everything we need."

"I like working," was Joseph's answer to that.

"You'll wear yourself out," said Mary anxiously.

"Of course I won't," replied Joseph, and smiled mysteriously.

He didn't tell Mary that he was saving up to buy her a donkey. That was going to be a surprise.

One day, Joseph realised that Mary was an unusually long time coming back from the water well. Although he still had a lot of work to do, he shook the wood shavings off his coat and went out into the street. As soon as he caught sight of Mary, he hurried towards her. She was sitting, utterly exhausted, at the side of the road. The big jug of water stood on the ground by her side.

"Dear Joseph," said Mary, "I was just having a bit of a rest and then I can go on carrying the water. Don't worry about me."

But Joseph lifted the jug and carried it in his arms – he couldn't carry it on his head like the women. How exhausting it was to carry the water! Mary followed him.

That night he took his money out and counted it. "I have to buy a donkey right now," he thought, but he said nothing to Mary.

Joseph went to the richest man in Nazareth. Anyone who owned so many donkeys could surely spare one of them.

"Will you sell me a donkey?" Joseph asked the rich man.

"Can you afford the price? A good animal costs a lot of money."

"Yes, sir," Joseph said with some hesitation. "How much do you want?"

But the rich man wanted much, much more money than Joseph had. He would have to work for many more months before he could earn so much money.

"Come back when you are able to pay," said the rich man.

"But I need one now. Mary is not strong and she can't carry everything herself. Couldn't I pay the balance later?"

"No," said the rich man. "I must have all the money now."

Joseph just stood there looking miserable and confused. But the rich man acted as though he were in a hurry.

"Goodbye," he said. "Come back when you're able to pay. Then we can do business."

And he turned to go. But Joseph held him firmly by his coat.

"Sir, don't you have just one donkey that is cheaper than the others?"

"No," said the rich man. "I have only the finest animals." Just then, though, he remembered the lazy, dirty donkey everyone laughed at. He would gladly get rid of that one. He certainly was a disgrace to the whole stable. All right, let this working man have that one for his money. "Just a moment," he said. "I do have one you could buy."

He called Simon and ordered him to bring the lazy donkey out.

Joseph waited eagerly. But when Simon arrived with the donkey, he saw straight away that this was not a good and reliable animal. It was the only one, though, that he could afford.

And so the rich man took the money, and Joseph took the donkey.

Then Joseph set out with the donkey on the long road home.

But the donkey thought that he had done enough work for that day, and he had no desire at all to go running about. He couldn't understand either why or where this strange man was taking him. So he resisted with all his strength.

In some places the path went up steps. When at last Joseph and the donkey reached the top the donkey suddenly pulled back and made Joseph let go of the reins. Then the donkey let himself slide back down the steps again, looking, as he did so, as if he was laughing. He often tried this trick on Simon, and Simon lost his temper whenever he managed it. But Joseph didn't get angry. He only sighed and spoke gently to him. "Just try to walk properly for once, or we won't get home before dark." And Joseph had to pull the obstinate creature up the steps again. "I'm afraid Mary will have more trouble than help with this beast," he thought sadly, as he wiped the sweat from his face.

At last they reached home. Joseph tied the donkey to an olive tree in front of the house and went in.

"I've bought a donkey for you, Mary," he said, but his voice sounded a bit sad.

"Oh, Joseph!" cried Mary. "You're so kind! Is that why you've been working so hard?"

"I wanted to get you a really good, hardworking donkey who would give you a lot of help. But I had only enough money for the laziest, dirtiest beast that ever trotted about on God's earth."

"Did you say lazy?" Mary asked eagerly. "Do you mean the donkey at the well? Does he move more beautifully than all the other donkeys, and does he hold his head higher than the others do? And is he really, really dirty?"

"Yes, he's dirty all right," Joseph said sadly. "I didn't notice if he moves beautifully. He's more inclined to sit on his backside and get himself pulled along."

But Mary was already outside. "Oh Joseph! It *is* him! Ever since you spoke to me about a donkey, this is just the one I wanted. But I never believed that my wish would come true. Thank you, thank you, dear, dear Joseph."

"But Mary," said the astonished Joseph, "why do you want simply the laziest, stupidest and dirtiest donkey in all Nazareth?"

"I'll tell you why," said Mary, who had already got a brush and started to groom the donkey. "Because he can become a splendid and very special donkey. Haven't you noticed what intelligent eyes he has? A donkey who walks so freely and lightly can certainly learn to carry a heavy load. Anyone who carries his head that high is surely noble and clean. It wasn't his fault that nobody groomed him. I'm so pleased with my donkey, Joseph. How can I ever thank you?"

"Perhaps you're right," Joseph said thoughtfully. "And I'm so pleased that you are happy. But let me groom him."

And Joseph groomed the donkey until he really shone. Mary stood at his side and gently patted him.

But the donkey was now utterly confused. What did all this mean? Why was he here with Mary? Anyway, he made up his mind to stay as long as possible. If they decided to send him back, they'd have to drag him away.

When Mary took the reins and said, "Come along!" he followed her willingly.

"This is where you'll sleep," Mary said.

She brought him an armful of sweet-smelling hay and put it in his manger. "Now eat and have a good sleep," she said, and she patted him. "Here is a new comrade for you," she explained to the sheep and goats in the stable. "Be nice to him."

Then Mary left, and the donkey felt agitated. "Baah," bleated the sheep. "Welcome. It's good to have a new comrade. And a donkey is just what Mary needs."

"Maah," bleated the goats. "Welcome! You understand that you're going to help Mary, don't you? We've been waiting a long time for you. It's good that you're here now."

This calmed the little donkey down. He was very surprised, because other animals had never been this friendly to him.

"What kind of stable is this?" he asked.

"It's Mary's, it's Mary's," cried all the lambs and the baby goats. "It's the best house in the world. Where do you come from, then?"

The little donkey didn't answer. He was just amazed, and happy.

"I'll never leave here," he decided.

All around him, the sheep and goats were sleeping now and soon the little donkey fell asleep too. But even in his deepest dream he went on thinking, "No, I'll never leave here, never..."

The great mystery

The little donkey woke early next morning. "What a happy dream I had in the night," he thought. "A strange man came and took me to Mary, who I really like. And the man said that I belong to Mary. And she was delighted, because she likes me too. I was brushed and combed until I looked lovely. Ah well, what a marvellous dream that was. The strange thing is, I'm still clean and tidy. It feels lovely, too, just like in the dream."

The little donkey cried "Hee-haw," which sounded as though he was trying to laugh.

It woke up the sheep and goats in the stable. "Good morning, little donkey," they said. "We hope you had a beautiful dream last night."

"Yes I did!" the little donkey answered. "I had the most beautiful dream in the whole world."

"That's wonderful," said the oldest sheep politely. "Look, Mary's coming."

All the animals jostled and pushed in their stalls, trying to be the first to greet Mary. They made quite a noise!

"Mary?" wondered the donkey, looking all round him. "I really am with Mary! That wasn't a dream at all. *It was true!*"

Quietly and patiently he stood and waited until Mary had stroked all the animals and given them something to eat. Last of all she came to the little donkey's stall.

"Good morning, my little donkey. Now, you have to eat well, so that you can grow big and strong. When I've milked the goats and taken them and the sheep to the meadow, we'll go and get water from the well. Until then, just go on munching your hay."

But the little donkey was so happy that he forgot to eat. Joseph came and looked at him too.

"He really does look handsome now," he marvelled. "You can hardly recognise him."

"Dear Joseph, he is the most beautiful donkey there is," said Mary.

"But I'm afraid you'll have a lot of trouble with him when you go to get the water," said Joseph. "You don't know how stubborn he is."

"If you can make him a yoke that fits well and doesn't rub, I'll fasten the water buckets to it and you'll soon see how good he is," Mary answered.

Joseph made what she wanted straight away. He measured

the donkey and went into the workshop. You could hear him working away busily with axe and plane. Then out he came, carrying a yoke that fitted the donkey's back.

"It rubs just a little on the right side. I can fix that," he said, and vanished again into his workshop. He came out with the yoke just as Mary finished her morning's work. When they placed it on the donkey's back, it fitted perfectly.

"Dear Joseph," Mary said gratefully, "no one can make as good a yoke as you."

The little donkey found that Mary was right. He had never had a yoke before that did not rub him and hurt him. This one was smooth and steady and comfortable.

Joseph fastened the water buckets to it.

"Goodbye, Joseph, we're going now," cried Mary, smiling happily.

"Goodbye," sighed Joseph. "I hope you can manage the donkey. I am very worried."

"There's no need to be," laughed Mary. "We'll be just fine. See how daintily he trots along." Joseph shook his head as he went back to his workshop.

Mary was proud and happy as she walked through the narrow, winding streets of Nazareth with her little donkey. She passed many low, square houses with flat roofs, and women and girls were coming out of every house carrying water jugs on their heads.

Mary went in front, with the donkey behind her. She just didn't believe that the donkey would be difficult and she didn't lead him at all. She had placed the reins over the yoke, and the donkey followed her like a good, obedient dog. Not once did he do anything wrong. How could anyone misbehave with Mary? When they reached the well, the women and girls gathered round the little donkey.

"Mary!" they said, "What a beautiful donkey. Where have you borrowed him from? He doesn't belong to you, does he?"

"Yes, he does. He belongs to me," Mary answered proudly. "Joseph bought him for me."

"Joseph?" they asked in surprise. "A beautiful animal like this? It must have been very expensive."

Mary just laughed. The girls stroked the donkey and praised his appearance. One of them picked red flowers and fastened them to his forehead.

"Look, Mary, now he could belong to a queen," this girl said. "I have never seen a donkey who holds his head so proudly."

Mary filled the water buckets and fastened them to the yoke.

"Let's go home," she said. "But take care that no water slops out."

The donkey went carefully and precisely, step by step, choosing the best place for his hoofs so that none of the fresh water would spill.

All this time, Joseph had been looking out for Mary and the donkey and he hurried out of his workshop as soon as they reached home.

"How did it go?" he asked. "Why are you back so soon? Was he so much trouble that you had to turn back? Just sit down, Mary, and have a rest. I'll go and deal with him."

"Joseph dear," Mary replied, "he is the best donkey in the whole world. I told you so before. We've been to the well. Look! The water is up to the brim and we didn't spill a drop."

Joseph was amazed. He gazed for some time at the water and then said: "All creatures are well behaved and gentle as lambs when you deal with them, because you are so good."

"I'm not good," Mary said, "but the little donkey is, and so are you, Joseph dear."

Mary then led the donkey out to the meadow, where the other animals were grazing.

"Thank you for helping me," Mary said. "Now have a good rest, my little donkey. You don't need to work any more today, but soon it will be harvest time and believe me, there'll be a lot to do then."

***

The meadow wasn't large but it was fine for the animals. A little stream flowed down from the mountains and along its banks grew green grass and tasty herbs. The air was full of a pleasant fragrance and a gnarled old olive tree gave some shade when the sun's heat was strongest.

Today, the animals told the little donkey a secret.

First of all they asked him if he wanted to hear the great secret.

Yes, of course he wanted to hear it.

Then they asked him if he could really keep the great secret to himself.

"Yes," he said, "I believe I can."

So they told him to listen. The oldest sheep drew a deep breath and began to speak. The donkey quivered with curiosity. But the younger sheep and the little goats, who knew already what was coming, grew so excited at the thought of the secret that they couldn't keep still. They started to jump, and to dance and to bleat. The large animals tried to calm them down but it was a long time before it was quiet enough at last for the oldest sheep to begin.

Trying again, she took a deep breath, and opened her mouth... but she was soon drowned by a whole flock of chirping and twittering birds. All the birds of Nazareth came flying by and settled in the large olive tree. They had heard the noise made by the young sheep and the little goats and realised at once that it was something to do with the great secret. They wanted to be there too. Even though they knew about it already, they had to sing wholeheartedly for joy whenever they thought about it. The old sheep had to wait until they were quiet. In the meantime, the poor donkey, though, had almost fainted with curiosity.

At last the sheep was able to speak. For the third time she took a deep breath and said, "Baa..."

But then the happy little grasshoppers began to chirp. In that country they are called cicadas and they too lived round the olive tree. This shrill chirping was a deafening sound to the donkey. But the cicadas thought it made a pretty tune, and besides, it was their nature to be happy.

When at last they stopped, the old sheep took a deep breath for the fourth time. She really wanted to speak of the secret solemnly and quietly, just as a secret really should be told, but instead she blurted it out very loud: "Mary is going to have a child: a son!"

At that she was interrupted again. The little sheep and goats gambolled and danced, the birds started to sing a new song and the grasshoppers chirped. The donkey, though, gave such a loud cry of joy, *"Hee-haw!"* that even the grasshoppers couldn't be heard any more.

It was a long time before the animals quietened down again.

Then it became very still. They were all thinking about Mary's child who would soon be born. Yes, now it was so silent that you could hear the gentle murmur of the stream.

The little sheep had suddenly become quiet. They stood there wondering what games they could play with the child. Perhaps he would like to play hide-and-seek round the old olive tree. The little goats were wondering if he would like to run races with them. The cicadas decided to teach the child how to chirp. The birds were composing lovely cradle songs. They knew that a little human child can't play and run straight away, but has to sleep a lot in order to grow and thrive.

Of course, the grown-up animals understood that too. The goats knew that the child needed good milk, and they were considering which plants they ought to eat to make their milk more nourishing than usual. They wanted to avoid bitter herbs and grasses so that their milk wouldn't be sour.

The sheep for their part reckoned that the little one would need soft, warm clothing and they were wondering if their wool would be delicate enough if they were careful and didn't let it get dirty.

But the little donkey had a wonderful idea. The small son of the rich man had a donkey with a saddle to ride. It always looked very smart when the boy came riding along. If only Joseph would make a child's saddle like that! From now on he would never behave badly with Joseph! He would be good and obedient. Perhaps Joseph would like him then, and give the child a saddle.

It was quiet for a long time. Everyone was thinking. Suddenly there was a frightened cry from a little lamb. "A snake!"

Right in the middle of the animals, close to the nose of the smallest lamb, lay a big snake, who lived far off in a corner of the meadow. How had he managed to get there, without anyone seeing him? They were all terrified!

Then the snake spoke and said: "You have been talking about Mary's child, and yet you are afraid of me. Don't you know that this child will be able to play with snakes without danger? Don't you know that he will care for wild and tame animals the same? Don't you know that on Mary's field, no living thing can harm any other?"

"Yes," answered the oldest sheep, very ashamed. "You are right. We won't be afraid of you any more. And you too can celebrate with us about Mary's child."

Harvest time

Harvest time came. There was lots and lots for Mary and her little donkey to do.

The figs had to be picked, carried home and laid out to dry on the flat roof. Mary's fig tree was bending under the weight of its fruit, and the baskets which the donkey had to carry were very heavy. But Mary patted him and gave him some sweet figs to chew, so he didn't feel tired. At last all the figs were gathered.

"Now, my little donkey, we can have a few days' rest before the vintage begins."

"Marvellous," the little donkey thought as he rubbed his head against Mary's arm. "I can spend the whole day in the meadow with the goats and sheep."

However next morning, Mary came into the stable with the yoke. "Little donkey," she said, "our poor neighbour Judith is all alone. She has no donkey. Let's give her a bit of help, you and I."

"It is marvellous in the meadow," the little donkey thought, "but it's even better to work the whole day with Mary."

And so he trotted off willingly with her. Judith was delighted to have help.

"I am old and weak," she said. "I didn't think that anyone still bothered about me. But I see that God thinks even about an old woman like me. And he has sent me the best woman in all of Nazareth."

"And the most intelligent donkey, Judith," laughed Mary.

Then Mary and the donkey worked for Judith for several days.

"We have finished now," Mary said one evening.

"I'll be able to spend tomorrow in the meadow for sure,"

thought the donkey. "That will be really wonderful. When I think about it, I know I really am a bit tired."

"The grape picking starts tomorrow," Joseph said when he came home. "It is too bad that you haven't had a good rest, Mary."

"It doesn't matter, Joseph," Mary answered. "After all, I have my hardworking donkey. If you hadn't bought him for me, I would have had to drag everything home myself, and then I would have been really tired. But I was able to help Judith and I'm very pleased that I could."

"What a pity," the oldest sheep said to the donkey. "You can't spend a single day enjoying yourself in the meadow."

"It really is wonderful in the meadow," the donkey replied, "but it is even more enjoyable to work with Mary."

"Oh yes, we all understand that," said all the animals.

***

The vintage was the jolliest time of the whole year. Everywhere, poor people in their little gardens and rich people in their great vineyards laughed and sang and picked the juicy grapes.

The animals all felt this happiness. Every day Mary's little donkey trotted along as though it was some sort of dance, although the baskets with the grapes were very heavy.

"What a lot of grapes we're getting this year," said Joseph. "And such beautiful ones too!"

"There's plenty, both for making wine and for drying," Mary replied happily. "But our little donkey is looking tired. He really must have a few days in the meadow to recover and get his strength back before the olive harvest begins."

"Tomorrow we're going to have fun in the meadow, aren't we?" cried the lambs and goats merrily.

"Yes, of course," said the donkey.

But early next morning Mary told her donkey: "Judith has nobody to help her pick her grapes. They are overripe already. She can't pick them fast enough any more. We must help her for a few days."

"It's lovely to be in the meadow," the little donkey thought to himself, "but it's nothing compared to working with Mary."

So he and Mary worked for poor Judith.

"How lucky I am to have good neighbours," Judith told them. "It is the best present God can give poor people."

Mary replied, "A hardworking donkey is a precious gift too."

And so Judith's grapes were picked and carried in too, and when that was done it was time for the olive harvest.

"You are not getting any rest," Joseph said.

"That doesn't matter," Mary assured him. "But I'm sorry for the donkey."

"No!" thought the donkey, and snuggled up to Mary. "There's nothing better in all the world than going with you."

"I must close my workshop for a few days and help too," Joseph declared.

***

The olive harvest was hard work. There was a small wood outside Nazareth where the old, gnarled olive trees grew and where all the Nazarenes had the right to pick olives. The men climbed to the top of the trees and struck down at the olives with long sticks; children collected them when they fell on the ground and they filled the baskets. The women picked the olives they could reach with their hands. Although the donkey now had to carry very heavy baskets, he never felt tired.

"You were right, Mary," Joseph said. "That is a really good donkey, the best in the whole town I do believe."

"He's the best in the whole world," insisted Mary.

Out in the olive grove, Mary's little donkey met the other donkeys of Nazareth. They didn't recognise him, not even the donkeys of the rich man. Neither did his old groom.

"What a splendid donkey," sighed the rich man's donkeys. "How delicately he trots along! How beautifully he holds his head up, so upright and proud! And how clean and well groomed he is!"

"He seems to me like a donkey I knew once," said the oldest donkey. "His walk and bearing were just as handsome. But I can't quite remember who it was."

"He is very handsome, very handsome," marvelled the youngest donkey. "And so strong."

And the old donkey declared: "He ought to be with us, because we belong to a really outstanding man. He isn't really suitable for these poor people."

"I just can't understand where they got him," wondered another.

Mary's little donkey heard all this and laughed to himself as he made his way home with the baskets. Many times he had to go to and fro between the olive grove and Joseph's house. And several times a day Joseph led the donkey past the house to Judith.

"Joseph, you must do that," Mary had said. "How else can the poor woman get her olives?"

"You're quite right," Joseph had agreed. "We have been given the best donkey in the whole world and to show our gratitude to God, the very least we can do is to help our neighbour. But time flies, and you are not getting any rest."

"It will soon be winter," said Mary. "I can take it easy then, and so can the little donkey."

"What does it matter if I have a rest or if I don't, just so long as I'm with Mary," the little donkey thought.

But when the harvest was over, the donkey had to go with Joseph.

***

The hot weather, which had parched the hills and the valleys, was over. It was getting colder. Joseph took the donkey with him into the countryside to collect firewood. Until late evening, Joseph searched for dry branches, which he tied on to the little donkey. Sometimes his load was higher than he was. They had to go a long way to find anything. There was only a little wood round Nazareth, and the other poor people of the town were out collecting wood too.

One day, when Joseph had gone unusually far with the donkey, black clouds began to gather in the sky. The sun was hidden and it became quite dark, although it was only early afternoon. A cold wind blew in from the sea.

"The rainy season is beginning," Joseph thought happily. "The earth won't be thirsty anymore. Every stream and every spring is filling with water again and the animals can drink as much as they like. This glorious rain!"

Unlike Joseph, the little donkey didn't like the rain. Ugh, no, it was unpleasantly wet and cold. Still, if Joseph said it was good, that must be right. All the same he longed to be home in his warm, dry stable. He pawed the ground impatiently.

"Now, now, little donkey," warned Joseph. "I think we should perhaps take a little more home today. Quite likely the rain will make us stay at home tomorrow. I know a place a little further north where we can certainly find some wood."

So the donkey had to go still further with Joseph. He was on the point of refusing to move. It occurred to him that it was fun to be disobedient, and to buck and rear. Joseph would find it a hard job to move him, he thought.

Suddenly he remembered the child. The child who, later on perhaps, would ride on his back. He must be obedient so that Joseph would make a pretty little saddle for him. So he trotted willingly along.

"You are a lovely, hardworking little donkey," Joseph praised him. "Perhaps you do understand that we have to gather a lot of firewood for Mary's sake. She must keep the house warm so that our little child doesn't freeze." At this the donkey felt ashamed of his ugly thoughts.

When they reached the place Joseph had spoken about, they found plenty of twigs. Joseph loaded up as much as the donkey could carry.

"Now we'll go back," said Joseph. "I'll walk beside you and hold the load steady."

Meanwhile, it was evening. The wind blew right through them, and it started to rain. It was a real cloudburst. The rain beat in their eyes so that they could hardly see anything. They advanced with difficulty. And then Joseph lost his way. He stood still and tried to pick out the path. It was impossible. Joseph and the donkey were lost.

"We must keep more to the left," Joseph thought and pulled the reins. But the little donkey wanted to go to the right. That was the way they had come. Why did Joseph want to go in the opposite direction?

"Come on!" cried Joseph and he pulled with all his strength.

Thereupon the little donkey sat down on his hind legs. Not a single step in the wrong direction!

"Don't turn stubborn now of all times," begged Joseph. "You have been so good and understanding. We must stick together if we're going to get home to Mary before night time."

That was just what the donkey wanted to do. But however much Joseph pulled, he remained rooted to the spot. Joseph let go of the reins for a moment in order to fasten some branches of wood which had become loose. The donkey was waiting for this. Quick as lightning he straightened up and trotted off to the right.

Joseph leaped after him and shouted, "Stop! We'll get lost. Stop!"

The donkey let Joseph come close enough to nearly get hold of him, and then trotted quickly away from him again. Joseph had to keep on following, although he was worn out and very worried. He was afraid he might lose Mary's little donkey.

Suddenly the donkey stopped and uttered a cry. In the darkness Joseph could hardly recognise him any more, but he heard his triumphant "Hee-haw!"

Joseph was finally able to grab his reins. He looked round and was utterly astounded. They were standing right in front of the town gate of Nazareth! "Well, I never!" Joseph thought. "Can I really believe my own eyes? We are in Nazareth! Mary was right. You are the most intelligent donkey in the whole world."

Mary was at home, sitting in the warm stable and milking the goats. The lambs and the goats gave her no peace. They nudged and jostled her, they pawed her knees with their hooves, all just to make her pat them and stroke them. The older animals tried to keep their young ones under control and told them off for troubling her.

"Don't stop them," Mary said. "They are so sweet and they'll grow quiet enough when they are older. And that happens very quickly. But where are Joseph and the donkey this evening? They must have been caught in the rain. I would be worried if I didn't know that the angels are protecting them."

At that very moment the stable door opened. Joseph and the donkey came in. Mary stood up and helped Joseph to unload the heavy wood and she dried the wet donkey. Joseph took off his soaking wet cloak and explained how he had lost the way and the donkey had found the right way and forced him to follow behind.

Mary laughed and said she had always known that her donkey was the cleverest donkey in the whole world.

And all the animals in the stable looked in wonder at the donkey and the oldest sheep said, "My children, there is a lesson for you all in this!"

"Yes," the lambs and goats bleated, "our donkey is very, very clever and a great hero."

"Oh, nonsense," the little donkey said. "I only wanted to get back to Mary as quickly as possible. That's why I took the right road home."

That night, just as every other night, the animals in the stable talked about Mary's little child. The donkey quickly forgot how very cold and tired he was.

"Isn't it coming soon, mother?" cried the lambs anxiously.

"Do you think it will come tomorrow?" bleated the impatient little goats.

"It will be a little while yet," answered the older animals.

"But only just a tiny little bit longer", said a little lamb excitedly. "A weeny, teeny little bit."

"Be good, children, and go to sleep now," commanded the oldest sheep. "Otherwise it will be a very long time indeed."

None of them dared to go on talking. The lambs and little goats dreamed about the child. But the donkey dreamed about Mary.

The Emperor's announcement

The next day it rained cats and dogs. The donkey was able to stay with his friends in the stable and rest. He thought it was marvellous to be able to rest at last.

In the evening Joseph came in when Mary was milking.

"Terrible weather!" he said. "It's a good thing we've managed to get everything in, all the harvest and the wood for the winter."

"Yes, we are lucky," Mary replied. "Joseph, do you think we could spare Judith a little wood?"

Joseph thought about this. "I think I could let her have one donkey load tomorrow. You are right, Mary. I will…"

Just then there was a loud knock on the door. Joseph went and opened it. He stayed outside for some time, and when he came back, he looked worried.

"Who was it?" Mary asked anxiously. "Was it something bad?"

"We must travel to Bethlehem immediately!" Joseph said.

"Bethlehem? That's a long way. What do we need to do in Bethlehem?"

"The Emperor has announced that all the people in his Empire have to be counted," explained Joseph. "Everyone is going to be written in big books and each man has to go to the town from which his family comes."

"But couldn't we be written just as well in the book here in Nazareth?"

"No, it has to be done in the town of each man's ancestors, because that is what the Emperor has ordered. I belong to the house of David in Bethlehem, and that's why we have to go there."

"But I can't go just now," Mary said. "The baby could be born any day."

The lambs suddenly became very excited, but neither Mary nor Joseph noticed.

"Shh!" warned the oldest sheep.

"The Emperor has ordered everyone to travel straight away," Joseph said. "We can't put off the journey."

"Joseph dear, then you must go alone. Surely you don't want the baby to be born by the roadside? Or among wild beasts in the wilderness?"

"Perhaps we can get to Bethlehem in time," said Joseph to comfort her.

"But," complained Mary, "we don't know anyone there we can stay with."

"I'm worried too, Mary," Joseph said gently. "But you must come with me. The Emperor has ordered that everybody must go. His scribes want to see every member of each family before they make an entry. And the Emperor must be obeyed!"

Mary sat down and thought about the problem. Suddenly she stood up and said, "It may be all right after all. We have our fine donkey, don't we? Who knows, perhaps God gave him to us just for this journey. I'll pack up all the child's things, and a warm fur for him to sleep in, and plenty of food for the journey. The donkey can carry all that and me too when I get tired."

"But who is going to look after all our animals while we are away?" wondered Joseph.

"I will go and see my sister tomorrow and ask her. Her husband is a Nazareth man, so they won't have to leave. She'll certainly look after the animals for us gladly, for as long as we're away. I believe everything is going to be all right, Joseph."

Mary went into the house and prepared supper. Joseph shut the stable carefully so that no wild animals could get in and steal the cattle. Then he too left the stable.

But the whole stable was in a state of shock. The animals had heard everything but without understanding it all. The lambs and little goats had only heard what Mary had said about the

33

child being born soon. The bigger animals had understood, though, that something was not quite right.

"It's going to come now, come now!" cried the small animals.

"But not here," replied the oldest sheep. "Joseph clearly said that they must go on a long journey, and that Mary had to go too."

"Well, the child can stay with us here," the little goats cried.

"I've never heard anything quite so stupid," grumbled the old sheep. "Mothers don't leave their children behind and go off on a journey. Anyway, the baby hasn't been born yet."

"Does Mary have to leave then, just when the baby is finally going to be born?" wailed the lambs and the little goats, who understood at last, although they still didn't want to believe it. "That isn't right."

"Be patient," the older animals advised. "Haven't you heard Mary say she would come back?"

"But that will take a long time," wailed the young ones.

"And what if they never find the way home again?" the youngest lamb asked.

"Our clever donkey will go with them," the oldest sheep answered. "So there is no danger of that."

"No, no danger," the little ones agreed. "But hurry as much as you can, little donkey."

"I will," the donkey assured them. "I'll go as carefully as possible too so that the baby isn't hurt at all. We'll soon be back, and then everything will be fine. Now go to sleep."

Gradually the lambs and little goats calmed down, and so did the big animals. Soon everyone in Mary's house, human and animal, was asleep.

For several days, Mary and Joseph worked very hard. The little donkey was allowed to stay in the stable most of the time.

"Have a thorough rest," Mary said. "It's a long, long way to Bethlehem."

Joseph completed all the orders he had for people in Nazareth. Then he delivered them to his customers. When that was done, he swept out the workshop, cleaned his tools and locked up.

Meanwhile, Mary baked bread and packed it up along with dry figs, olive oil and other good food in a hamper.

Then she put together all the things she had sewn for the baby, the shawl, the blankets to wrap him in, and the little clothes. How delicately beautiful they were! She spread them all out on the table and looked at them. She called Joseph to come and admire them. Then she bundled them all up in a white sheepskin.

When she was ready to leave, Mary brushed and mended her own and Joseph's clothes so that they would both be neat and clean when they travelled to strange places.

She visited her sister, of course, and asked her to look after the animals. Her sister was very sad that Mary had to leave Nazareth and she gladly agreed to take care of the animals. Even old Judith offered to help.

"I had always hoped I would be able to rock your son in his cradle, but instead of that I'll look after your lambs."

"Thank you, Judith," Mary replied. "That makes me very happy."

On the last evening before she left, the animals pressed more strongly against Mary than usual when she sat down and was going to milk them.

"My dears," Mary said, "do you know that I have to go away? I see it in your eyes. Don't be sad. My sister has promised to be good to you. And so has old Judith. Besides, Judith has plenty of time: she can tell you plenty of stories and spoil you, because she has nothing else to do. My sister is always in too much of a hurry to do that."

Then all the animals bleated, but they sounded dreadfully miserable and sad.

"Now, listen," said Mary. "I'll come back soon. And then, oh, I'll be carrying my little son in my arms. Listen, you little ruffians, you'll have to be careful then, and not push and shove, because he'll be small and delicate, and you mustn't hurt him. Now be really good all the time I'm away. But you must learn to wait patiently, because it will certainly be a long time."

Mary said goodbye to them that evening. "You won't be awake tomorrow morning when we leave," she said.

But they were all awake, all of them, and they watched Joseph miserably while he loaded the donkey and fastened all the baggage safely on him.

"Don't be sad," the little donkey said comfortingly to his friends, "we are going away now, but we'll soon come back."

"Take good care of Mary and her baby," urged the animals.

"I promise," the donkey answered seriously.

"Come on now," Joseph said and he lifted Mary into the saddle. "We must be off. It's still dark, but it'll soon be light. Wrap your shawl around you tightly, Mary, because the wind is cold this morning."

And so Joseph, Mary and the little donkey set out on the long journey to Bethlehem.

On the road to Bethlehem

It was a long way from Nazareth to Bethlehem. It took the little donkey nearly a whole week, although he trotted along brightly from early in the morning to late in the evening.

The donkey was proud, though, of being able to carry Mary on his back all day, and with head held high he trotted along as gracefully and spiritedly as ever.

"Joseph, I am so pleased with our donkey," Mary said. "I couldn't have gone all this way without him. What a good thing it was that you bought him for me."

For the first few days the road went through places they knew. They went past the fields and pastures, the vineyards, olive orchards and fig-tree plantations of Nazareth. Then they came to strange villages, but these were very similar to Nazareth.

Sometimes it poured with rain. Mary and Joseph were glad when it rained, because plenty of rain is good for both plants and animals. Sometimes the sun shone, and they were glad that they could dry their wet clothes and warm their cold, frozen arms and legs.

In time they came to a stream which had burst its banks after heavy rain. Usually it was just a narrow little stream which could easily be crossed. But today it was a wide, roaring torrent!

Joseph was worried and stood and stroked his beard thoughtfully.

How could they get across?

He gathered his long cloak up. Then he cautiously advanced one step into the water. Woosh! The stream could easily have dragged him along. Joseph quickly pulled himself back on to the bank.

"I wish I knew what to do," Joseph was thinking. "I don't think the donkey can cross there! We'll have to wait until the water subsides. But that could take days."

"I believe that God will show us a way," Mary said confidently. "Joseph, look at our donkey!"

The little donkey suddenly began to dance along the bank, with Mary still on his back. He had seen a shining figure which beckoned him, and he was following it. It was an angel, but neither Joseph nor Mary could see it.

When the donkey reached the angel, the angel grasped the reins and led the donkey into the water.

"Stop! Stop! Donkey!" shouted the terrified Joseph. "Pull him back, Mary!"

But the donkey was wading strongly through the water. The angel guided him to the opposite bank over some large, flat stones. Joseph couldn't see the stones, of course, because the water was pouring over them, but he rushed after the donkey and reached the opposite bank just as safely.

"Mary," he cried, "were you very frightened?"

"Frightened?" Mary asked in surprise. "Why should I be frightened? I believe the angel of God was guiding the donkey, although I couldn't see him."

"You may well be right," said Joseph. "It really was stupid of me to be so afraid. How my heart pounded!"

***

Soon it was midday. Mary dismounted from the donkey. They ate and rested under a fig tree, which had many new buds. Joseph found some winter figs to eat and gave them to Mary.

"You see," Mary said. "This rain really suits these trees. They don't look so dry and withered any more. There is new life in them."

Just at that moment the air became full of the joyous song of many birds. A flock of birds had settled in the tree and were singing with all their heart.

"How happy they sound," Mary said. "Can you hear them singing about my child?"

Joseph laughed. "How do you know that?"

"I just know," Mary said mysteriously. "But Joseph, haven't you noticed? They're our birds."

"Our birds?"

"Yes, don't you recognise them? They're the birds from our garden in Nazareth. That one is the little one who always jumps sideways, and there's the tame one, look, who isn't afraid to eat out of my hand. Don't you recognise them, Joseph? And I know that one too! And that one, and that one! Yes, they are all there. Oh, Joseph, they've flown after us. They want to be there to meet the baby."

"Are you quite certain that they're our birds?" asked Joseph, who felt that he recognised them too.

"Quite sure," Mary said. "That's right, isn't it, my little donkey? You recognise them too, don't you?"

Yes, the little donkey recognised them. He had noticed for a long time that they were following. Sometimes they had flown on ahead, sometimes they kept behind, and sometimes they were sitting on a tree and chirping as the donkey trotted by, and occasionally they flew along close to Mary. The donkey only wondered why Mary had not recognised them earlier.

After resting they all travelled on until it was evening. It was hard to keep going for so many hours. All three were tired out when the sun set.

"We shouldn't go any further today," Joseph declared. "We must look for somewhere where we can spend the night."

"In a house if possible, Joseph," Mary pleaded.

"Are you cold? Perhaps we can manage to keep going a bit longer and reach a village soon," Joseph said.

***

It was getting dark quickly as they struggled on, and Joseph was afraid that they wouldn't find a house and would be forced to spend the night in the open after all.

"Don't worry, Joseph," Mary said. "I believe that God will help us."

She had hardly spoken these words when an angel again appeared to the donkey and beckoned him. The donkey ran towards him and on to a small hillock. From there a faint light could be seen quite near them.

"Joseph, a village! God be praised!" cried Mary happily.

The travellers soon reached the village. Joseph knocked at the door of the first house and asked for shelter. The people of the house were quite poor. The husband invited them to come in, and the wife invited them to share supper.

Soon Mary, Joseph and the donkey were fast asleep in the strange house.

In the morning they were all awakened by the singing of the birds.

"What birds are those?" the man asked.

"They are my birds," Mary told him. "They flew along with us because they want to welcome my child with their happy song the moment he comes into the world."

"Birds from Nazareth?" asked the man in astonishment.

"What kind of a child is going to be born then," asked the woman, "if the birds fly such a long way just to sing at his birth? Is there something special about this child?"

Mary smiled and nodded mysteriously.

"You must visit us again and show us the child on your way back," urged the woman.

"Gladly," Mary said.

Meanwhile the children of these poor people had made friends with the little donkey. They had helped Joseph to groom him, had given him hay and water and didn't want to be parted from him. One small boy started to cry. "Mother, why can't we buy a donkey like this," he sobbed.

"We can't do that," said his mother. "But when you're big enough, you can earn enough money yourself to buy one."

"But we want to have him now and ride him sometimes," wailed the boy.

The other children didn't speak. They all stood round the little donkey shyly and stroked him wherever they could touch him.

"Let the little ones come a short way with us," Joseph suggested, "and then they can have a little ride."

Their mother laughed and agreed.

How happy they were!

Joseph lifted the smallest child up to Mary and the whole group moved forward, singing and shouting with joy. Joseph let the oldest boy lead the donkey and he followed on behind.

After a while Mary gave the smallest child to her sister and lifted up the boy who had cried so sadly before. Now he boldly clicked his tongue to make the donkey go faster, and

was so excited and playful that Mary had trouble holding onto him.

All the children had their turn riding the donkey. They had gone a really long way from their home before they had finished. The group rested then and Mary let the little ones share her morning snack.

"Now we have to send you all home so that your parents don't start to worry," Mary declared.

"We have never had so much fun," said the oldest sister. "Mary is so lovely."

"So is the donkey," cried the cheeky small boy.

"And Joseph," they all agreed.

"Will you really come back?" they asked. "Can we travel along with you again?"

Joseph promised that they would.

"Can I lead the donkey then?" the small boy asked. "By that time I'll have grown a whole lot bigger."

"Yes," Joseph said, "you can lead him quite a long way."

"I'll collect some juicy grass for him every day," the little boy declared, "a really big heap. That's how good a time you'll have with me, little donkey."

"With us too," the others assured him.

The oldest sister shyly asked, "When you return, will you let me hold the baby?"

"Certainly. I have noticed how well you treat your smaller brothers and sisters. See that they all get home safely. Otherwise I shall worry about you all. You have a long way to go to reach home now."

At last the children said goodbye and left. But for as long as Joseph, Mary and the donkey could see them, they were walking backwards and waving.

***

Towards evening, the travellers came to a very quiet, lonely area. The villages were a long way from each other.

"I'm afraid that we'll have to spend tonight in the open," Joseph said sadly. "From here we have a good view in all directions but I can't see any lights whichever way I look. Do you think you will get really cold?"

"As long as it doesn't start to rain," Mary replied, "it will be all right. But, it is a clear, starry night. Although the wind is cold, we can wrap ourselves up in the shawl."

Joseph helped Mary down from the donkey. She sat down by the side of the road and Joseph saw that she was shivering with cold. He took off his cloak and put it round her.

"Don't," said Mary. "You're just as freezing as I am."

"Keep it to begin with," Joseph pleaded. "I'll look around for somewhere sheltered from the wind."

43

"Yes, I'm sure God will let us sleep well tonight too," Mary said. "But hold on, where is the donkey?"

"Hee-haw!" came the answer out of the darkness.

Once more the donkey had caught sight of an angel, who had shown him a cave quite nearby. It was obvious that travellers often spent the night there as there was some straw on the ground and one or two dry logs by a burnt-out fireplace. How delighted Joseph was when he saw in the pale light of the stars what the donkey had discovered. He got Mary and piled up straw to make her a bed. He made fire, and lit one or two logs. It was warm and comfortable in the dark cave.

"God really does protect us, Joseph," said Mary. "Every night we find a bed, even in the middle of the wilderness."

They slept peacefully and safely until the birds woke them at sunrise.

In the robbers' den

Day after day Joseph, Mary and their little donkey travelled along the road to Bethlehem. Sometimes things looked bad for them, but each time the angel showed the little donkey what to do.

But one time, the donkey gave them a fright.

The travellers were making their way through a lonely area. Early in the afternoon they came to a village. They drew water from the well and while they were resting Joseph said, "Do we want to go any further today? I'm afraid that it's a very long way to the next place. We might not reach it before dark."

"But don't you think that it's still too early to look for a place to spend the night?" Mary answered. "The nearer we are to Bethlehem the better it is for us."

"Let's ask this woman," Joseph said, and he stopped a woman who was walking by.

"If you keep up a good speed you could reach the next village before nightfall," the woman said and looked at them with curiosity. "But the road is difficult, steep and very stony. Ah, but your donkey looks strong, he should be able to make it."

"He is the best donkey in the world," said Mary.

"But there are robbers along the road," the woman added. "They live in the wild mountains. They are very dangerous if you fall into their hands. Perhaps you'd better wait until tomorrow. Some people from this village are going to Jerusalem, and you could join them. The robbers don't dare to attack if there are a lot of people."

"Yes," agreed Joseph, "it probably is best for us to wait. Is it quite certain that these people will be travelling tomorrow?"

"I think so," answered the woman. "Or, maybe the day after tomorrow."

"Shouldn't we try then to reach the next place?" Mary said. "It is still quite early in the afternoon. Our little donkey is reliable. And God will protect us from the robbers."

***

So they travelled on. It had been such a beautiful day when they set out but an hour or so later the wind suddenly whipped up and a heavy shower took them by surprise. In a moment it became completely dark, just at the most difficult part of the road.

The donkey had to go on ahead with Mary and had to feel carefully with his hoofs for the safest path. Joseph climbed behind them, because the road was very narrow.

"We must find some shelter," cried Joseph. "This wind is blowing right through you."

But the donkey didn't find any shelter and Mary began to freeze with cold.

"We must stop soon, even if we don't come to any houses," Joseph was thinking.

Before his very eyes the donkey suddenly disappeared. He had to run to catch up with him.

Once more the donkey had seen an angel. The angel beckoned him to the far side of a gigantic boulder. A narrower path ran along there and a little way along it the donkey came to a hut.

"Joseph! There's a hut here!" Mary called, and tried to turn round in his direction. Joseph was running along behind them, breathing hard.

The donkey was already close to the hut. It was only a rickety shack without a door. But a fire was burning on the floor and three men sat round it, warming themselves. When they caught sight of the donkey one of them jumped up, seized the reins and led the donkey into the hut.

How delighted the donkey was that in this terrible weather, Mary at last had a roof over her head.

"Thank you, you're very kind," said Mary. "Do you mind if we warm up a little by your fire? We are wet through."

The men didn't answer at first.

Mary didn't look at them at all carefully, because her eyes were on the fire and she stretched her hands out towards it. But Joseph, who came in at this moment, saw what kind of people these three men were. Their little donkey had led them right into the robbers' den!

"Please," Mary asked them, "we don't want to give you any trouble, but please let us just sit by your fire."

"Come on then," one of them said roughly.

Mary stretched her hands out towards him and so he had to help her down from the donkey's back. And at that moment he had the feeling that the fire burnt more brightly and the air in the shack had the fragrance of a spring day. Mary sank down on the straw on the floor. Joseph still hesitated at the door. He didn't know what to do for the best.

"Joseph, pass me down the box with the food," Mary asked him. "You must be hungry too."

Joseph got the food and Mary took out the loaf. She broke it in pieces and said, "Lord, bless our bread!"

She passed a piece of bread to Joseph and gave some to the three robbers. The three men were so embarrassed that they could hardly eat. It was a very long time since they had eaten bread that had been blessed!

Mary and Joseph ate and the little donkey started to nibble at the straw on the floor.

The three robbers continued to sit still and watch the strangers. They couldn't understand how anyone could find their hidden shack. All the same, it was useful to have people coming straight to them. All they had to do was to take their luggage while they were sleeping and then sneak out with the donkey. There was no need to use force at all.

The three robbers looked and winked at each other. Joseph realised what sort of people they were. He looked worried and could hardly swallow his food. But Mary seemed quite unaware. She looked at the robbers with wonderfully bright eyes and smiled at them as if they were good, old friends.

When she had finished eating Mary dried the donkey and said, "You don't know what a clever donkey this is!"

And she started to tell them how the donkey had waded across the river that had burst its banks and how he found a resting place for them every night.

"But this evening we had started to think that we were going to spend the night in the open. It was surely an angel who showed our little donkey the path. Without an angel we would never have found this hut right out in these lonely mountains," she told them.

The robbers listened to her in astonishment. They thought that this was a very childish woman. What angel would have led their donkey into a robbers' hide-out, of all places. She must be easy to fool.

Then an idea came to the robber chief which struck him with terror. He became quite pale and broke out into a cold sweat.

There was something unusual about this woman and he had noticed this from the beginning. When he helped her down from the donkey, everything near her had been bright and lovely. It wasn't the fire that had burnt brighter, although that was what he had believed at first! No, he knew what it was now. Another being had been with her, and from this other being the light and warmth had poured out. An angel. And after that, he had sat there making wicked plans against people who were watched over by an angel! He went cold at the thought of what would have happened to him and his comrades if they had lifted a hand against these people. Luckily the woman had spoken before they had been able to do her any harm. He must see to it that his comrades left these strangers in peace.

The two other robbers laughed mockingly as they listened to the lively, innocent story of the woman.

Then a bird chirped quite unexpectedly. Mary interrupted her story and cried out, "Listen, Joseph! Our birds have found the way here!"

And then she began to tell the even more miraculous story of the birds of Nazareth. She told them how the birds had flown after her for the whole journey so that they could meet her child as soon as he was born into the world. Whenever they rested the birds sat in a tree and sang for her, and every morning they woke her with a song.

The men thought the woman was unbelievably childish, but they couldn't help listening to her. And when they looked up, they saw that the beams and rafters were full of sleeping birds.

The second robber was a rough fellow. He had no respect for anything and hit out without mercy to get whatever he wanted. But as a small boy he had been crazy about birds and he had always been very good at handling them.

He stared at Mary's birds like a man bewitched. Hardly aware of what he was doing, he collected some breadcrumbs and held them out in his outstretched hand. Then he whistled softly. One or two heads came out from hiding under their wings. Two or three birds flew out and circled round him, but they were uneasy. They looked at Mary as though asking her advice. Should they? Mary nodded. The boldest one, the little one who hopped sideways, flew on to the robber's hand and pecked at a tiny crumb. In a flash he had the whole flock round him. They settled on his hands, on his shoulders and on his head, twittering and chirping.

The robber sat quite still, so as not to scare them away.

"How I have longed for birds," he said. "For birdsong. Here in the mountains you only hear the vulture's shriek."

"Do you like these birds?" Mary asked.

The robber became friendly then and asked Mary and Joseph the names of the birds and where they made their nests and how many little ones they usually had, and a whole lot more. He wanted to know more than they could tell him.

"I can't understand," he thought, "why I have stayed so long in these barren mountains. Tomorrow I'm going to go to some place where there are trees and birds. I'll stay there and earn my living with the work of my hands. If it wasn't for these strangers with their birds, I would have stayed here till my dying day. I am so glad you came. I will see to it that my comrades leave you in peace. Birds have always made me so happy!"

The youngest robber hadn't asked about angels or birds. He was quite young, and had only come across the other two not long before. He came from a good home but had always been wild and unruly. He always wanted to come first and to be the best. And one day someone else in his village won something instead of him. In his rage he left the village and joined the robbers, to make a name for himself as "Terror of the Wilds". He was going to show the people of his village! They were going to fear him and tremble when they heard his name! He had always been very wild and fierce when he and his companions were looting and robbing.

Now he sat and grew angry with his comrades. He saw clearly that they were both being charmed by the strange woman and thinking of having mercy on her and her husband.

"You poor old fools!" he thought angrily. "Soon you too will be like children again and too weak to go robbing any more. All right, that doesn't matter. Tonight when everyone is sleeping I'll take the baggage and the donkey and disappear."

Then he began to imagine what could be in the bags. Something valuable, for sure.

He could feel that, in some way or other, the strangers were unusual. Quite likely they were not as poor as they seemed. The woman had a well-bred look. Now he realised what it was. She was in disguise. She probably thought that she could carry her jewels through the countryside more safely if she looked like a beggar woman and hid everything in a rough bundle. But he saw through it all! They couldn't fool him! And this donkey certainly did not belong to poor people! No!

There were some very valuable things in that bundle, he was sure. And tomorrow it would all belong to him! Once he was a long way away, he was going to open it and be a rich man. And then he was going to collect a gang of wild daredevils round him and be a robber chief. The "Terror of the Wilds"! They'd hear about him at home in his own village! If only these people would lie down and go to sleep. Sitting up and chattering the whole night!

He was so full of impatience that he was biting his nails all the time. Ah, well, it would soon be quiet.

But once more the oldest robber could not stay silent. "Who are you really?" he asked Mary. "Birds fly after you, but an angel leads your donkey straight into a robbers' den."

"I am only Mary of Nazareth," Mary explained, "and Joseph is simply Joseph. It's not for our sakes that the birds fly after us and the angels protect us. It's for the sake of the child who is going to be born soon."

"A baby?" whispered the old robber.

Mary nodded and smiled at him. And at that moment, the fear that had filled him at the appearance of the angel left him. He felt well and happy.

"Wonderful," he thought.

"Here, I'll show you something really beautiful," Mary said mysteriously to the robber. "Joseph, please help me to get the bags down."

Joseph undid the straps. The youngest robber held his breath in his excitement. His right hand clutched the handle of his dagger so fiercely that his knuckles were quite white.

What kind of jewels did this woman have? What was she so proud of?

She sat down and put the bundle on her lap. When she had brushed all the pieces of straw from her dress she took out one or two small child's clothes and showed them to the astonished robbers.

"Look!" she said and passed one to each of them. "Aren't they just perfect?"

The youngest robber was so taken aback that he let his dagger fall to the ground.

Joseph saw it and quick as lightning pushed it with his foot into the straw. But the robber didn't notice this at all. He stood there, twisting and turning the little baby's garment this way and that, and getting redder and redder in the face.

What a disgrace! Supposing he had stolen this bundle with the little child's clothes! There would have been laughter from town to town, from village to village. Even the smallest child would have laughed at the mere mention of his name. The "Terror of the Wilds", who stole the clothes of a newborn baby!

He threw the little garment into Mary's lap. Mary carefully folded the child's clothes up again. Everyone was silent.

Then the young man started to speak. "I wanted to be a hero. But you don't become famous for stealing the clothes of a baby who has not yet been born. Tell your child when he grows up that the 'Terror of the Wilds' was planning to steal his baby clothes. Then he'll know how evil men are."

"My son is coming to help those who have taken a wrong path," Mary said.

"Tell him this," the young man cried. "Yes, yes, I'll make a fresh start and become an honest man. You can't win fame and honour as a robber. 'Terror of the Wilds' Ha! How stupid I've been."

"I'll come with you," said the old robber.

"I don't want to stay here any longer either," said the man with the birds. "I'd already made up my mind to go somewhere where there are trees and the song of birds."

"Mary of Nazareth," said the old robber, "tell your child that because of him, the three most evil robbers left these barren mountains and set out to become good human beings."

"I shall tell him," Mary replied smiling, "that three good men took pity in a terrible storm on two travellers and their little donkey."

Then they all slept quietly through the night in the robbers' den. And next morning the birds of Nazareth sang for three happy men who were not robbers any more.

"I'll show you the best way to the next village," the young man said.

He took the donkey's reins and led him along an almost hidden path until a village could be seen in the distance.

"Thank you, Mary's little donkey, for coming to us last night," he said.

He stroked the donkey and gave him a farewell pat and said goodbye to Mary and Joseph. They wished him good luck. After that he returned to his comrades who were already packing their few belongings for the journey to another country.

With the shepherds

"Mary," Joseph said that day, "do you know, I think we'll reach Bethlehem tomorrow, if all goes well."

"That would be marvellous," sighed Mary. "The baby is not going to wait much longer. It will be good to have a roof over our heads again."

"Aha," thought the little donkey, "if that's how things are, I must hurry." And he started to trot, trot along so that Joseph had to run beside him to keep up.

"It's remarkable that our donkey is so strong still," Mary said thoughtfully. "He had to work so hard all through the harvest and yet he has carried me for days, from dawn to dusk on his back."

"Yes... yes," said Joseph, breathing heavily. "I don't know... how... he... keeps... going."

They travelled on past fields and again and again they came across large flocks of sheep and herds of goats. They saw no houses, only little huts for the shepherds and low stone pens in which the animals spent the nights.

Joseph stood in front of one of these stone walls that evening. Many, many animals had been herded together and were lying close to each other side by side. The shepherds had made a fire and were sitting by it and warming themselves. One of them kept watch. He had wrapped himself in a sheepskin and was lying right across the middle of the entrance. Anyone who wanted to go in had to step over him. But anyone who tried to do this would be chased away. This would happen to whoever came at night, whether it was a wild animal who wanted to carry off sheep, or a thief who wanted to steal goats.

Joseph approached the entrance. The shepherd stirred warily.

"What do you want?" he asked gruffly.

"May we spend the night with you? We can't manage to reach Bethlehem."

"Yes," said the shepherd after looking carefully at Joseph from head to foot. "Come in. We have no tent, only a fire. You'll have to be content with that..."

He stood up and led Joseph, the donkey and Mary in.

A twelve-year-old boy came running towards them. "Let me look after the donkey," he said eagerly. "What a lovely animal. But he's very wet. Has he been sweating?"

"Yes, he has been in such a hurry all day," explained Joseph and he dried his own forehead. "It's good that we can rest now."

The boy rubbed the donkey down with dry grass, gave him hay and fresh water, stroked him, spoke quietly to him and looked after him in every way as well as he could. When he saw that he was freezing in the cold night air, he took his own cloak off and spread it over the donkey's back.

"Reuben, what are you doing?" called his grandfather.

"The little donkey is very cold. He was very wet with sweat," the boy replied. "I don't need a cloak. I'm never cold."

His grandfather shook his head and told him to come to the fire and sit down.

Reuben obeyed him and the old man wrapped his own cloak round the boy.

When the shepherds noticed how tired and cold Mary was, they said, "You can't spend the night lying on the open ground. It is going to be cold tonight, the stars are shining unusually brightly."

One of the shepherds had already brought one or two goatskins and they all helped to make a small, warm tent with them, a tent just big enough for Mary. Inside the tent they spread a sheepskin on the ground, and another shepherd brought some goat's milk. Mary accepted all these things very gratefully. Then she lay down on the soft sheepskin and fell asleep immediately. She was too tired that evening to sit up and talk as she had done the previous evening in the robbers' den.

But Joseph sat with the shepherds by the fire for a long time. He told them all about their journey and their adventures. The shepherds listened very attentively, and when he told them how an angel had always shown the donkey the right way, they nodded solemnly.

"Did you see the angel?" they asked.

"No, neither I nor Mary. But she was aware of it, whenever an angel was close."

"Yes," the old man said thoughtfully. "Good people can feel the presence of an angel, although they can't see him."

"Our forefathers often talked to angels," another man remembered.

"The angels have helped us until now," said Joseph, "and we hope they will guide us to Bethlehem too, before Mary's child comes into the world."

"In Bethlehem," explained the old grandfather proudly (for he and all the shepherds came from there) "in Bethlehem King David was born. He guarded his father's flocks as a boy, and when he grew up he became the King and Shepherd of the whole nation."

"We are all part of his family line," Reuben's father added.

"We are too," said Joseph. "And that's why we have to go to Bethlehem. We are to be counted there."

"Yes, indeed," said another shepherd and he added, "David was born in Bethlehem, but we are still waiting for another King; he was promised to our forefathers by God."

"Reuben, tell us what the prophet says about the child of Bethlehem," urged his grandfather.

"From you, O Bethlehem, shall come forth for me one who is to be ruler over my people," rang out Reuben's clear voice.

"It has also been written," said Joseph softly, "that he will be the Good Shepherd."

"Who shall lead all people along God's path," added Reuben eagerly.

"Yes," one of the shepherds said. "That has been written. But he never comes, although we need him. The years come and go and everything stays the same."

The old grandfather spoke again. "It has always been my strong desire to live to see the child of Bethlehem. It is now unfortunately too late for him to come in my lifetime."

All the shepherds sighed. They had eagerly awaited the Good Shepherd for a long time.

Reuben said shyly, "Do you know what, Grandfather, I believe he is coming soon. I can feel it."

"Little boy," the old man replied, "how can you know that?"

"Because something very strange happened just now," said Reuben. "When I was spreading my cloak over the donkey's back, his eyes had a strange gleam. I've never seen anything like it, and I was astonished. But then I noticed the stars were mirrored in his eyes. I turned round and looked up into the sky and the stars were shining so brightly you could almost hear them. It really was like that. And I believe they were singing, "Soon! Soon! Soon!" Then I looked at the donkey again. He knew too that something will happen soon. The Good Shepherd is coming now, I'm certain."

"Reuben, be careful not let your imagination get the better of you," the boy's father said sternly.

"Who knows, Reuben may be right," his grandfather suggested. "The stars certainly are unusually bright tonight."

After that there was quiet around the fire. One after another the shepherds wrapped themselves in their cloaks and fell asleep.

Only the little donkey was unable to sleep. He was so excited by Mary's words, that the child would soon be coming. She really didn't have the time to spend the whole night resting here, letting hour after hour slip by.

"Little donkey, why are you standing there stamping your hoof?" a sheep asked. "Why don't you sleep?"

"I can't," sighed the donkey. "I can't help thinking all the time about Mary's baby. We have waited for it a long time already, you know, and today she said that it would not make her wait any longer. Besides, I promised the other animals at home that I would carry Mary safely and in good time to Bethlehem. Suppose we don't get there... Just imagine the child being born by the roadside! If only I could wake Joseph and Mary up and hurry on with them."

"The night is too dark," remarked another sheep, who had been listening.

"The angels would show me the way."

"Have you seen an angel tonight?" argued the first sheep. "Has one beckoned you? If one had, you would have had to follow immediately."

"No," admitted the donkey. "No, I haven't seen one."

"Then the angels must think that you should rest here for the night," the sheep said.

"Yes, and look how warm and comfortable the shepherds have made everything for the woman."

"Yes, and see how soundly she is sleeping," added another sheep. "And her husband is sleeping too. He too needs sleep, he was very tired when he arrived here."

"Yes," sighed the donkey, "you are right. I only hope they wake up in good time."

***

They were all up early the next morning. The shepherds invited Joseph and Mary to their early morning meal, and the little donkey was given an armful of hay by Reuben. The birds of Nazareth sang their happiest morning song.

"Now, you haven't far to go to reach Bethlehem," Reuben's grandfather said. "You'll be there by midday. You'll find it hard though to find somewhere to stay. A large number of people from David's family line have come because of the Emperor's order. All the same, I expect you'll be all right. And when you come back along this road, we hope you'll pay us a visit, because we're eager to see the child who is to be born in Bethlehem. A child of the line of David!"

Mary gladly promised to do this.

"And I'll have hay and fresh water ready again then for your donkey," Reuben promised. "He is the finest donkey I know."

"You are a good boy, Reuben," Joseph said. "May God be with you always."

Then Joseph and Mary said goodbye to the shepherds and travelled on.

But on this day, they had a lot of bad luck.

First of all, there was cold rain and they were soaked right through. After the rain the sky remained cloudy and grey for the rest of the day. No sun broke through to dry their clothes and warm their frozen limbs.

Then the little donkey had an accident. He had slept badly and was tired. When he was clambering up a steep hill, which was covered with a mass of slippery stones, he slipped and nearly fell. Mary cried out, but the donkey was just able to keep

59

his balance and go on climbing. Walking on his foot hurt. Mary and Joseph soon noticed that he was limping.

"You poor thing," Mary comforted him. "You have carried me now for such a long time. We'll soon be there, though, and then you can have a rest."

The donkey trotted along as well as he could, although not as fast as usual. Joseph had no trouble in keeping up with him this day.

They reached Bethlehem in the afternoon. The town was surrounded by a wall, and travellers could only enter through a gate. A watchman sat in the gateway and Joseph had to tell him his name, Mary's name, where they came from and what their business was before he let them through.

Then, at last, they were in Bethlehem.

"Oh Joseph, I'm so happy," Mary said. "Praise the Lord, that we are finally here. And thank you, my wonderful little donkey. It has been hard and difficult for you, but you were so good."

"He's worth his weight in gold," said Joseph, feeling very glad. "We would never have made it without him."

The donkey felt so proud and happy.

"Hee-haw!" he cried, and looked round for the birds of Nazareth.

They were all sitting in a row on the town wall.

"You have done very well, little donkey," they chirped.

The stable

Joseph and Mary soon discovered that Bethlehem was a town with houses as small and streets as narrow as Nazareth. But which way should they go to find somewhere to stay?

They set off at random and soon came to an inn. "They rent rooms here to travellers," explained Joseph. "Wait, I'll ask them if we can stay here."

But when he went in he found that every room was occupied. Not even the smallest corner was free. It was too full.

"We'll go to the next inn," Joseph said to Mary. "There are several, I'm sure."

They went on looking in one narrow street after another.

"My wife is tired, and her baby might be born at any moment," Joseph said each time he came to an inn.

And all the landlords gave the same answer: "Impossible. Try somewhere else."

When they had tried everywhere, Joseph suggested, "Perhaps a family will take us in."

"I am worried most about our little donkey," Mary sighed. "Look, how badly he is limping! He needs a good rest."

"Let's try this house," Joseph said and he knocked.

"Kind friend, can you put us up for the night," Joseph asked. "We have only just arrived in Bethlehem, but there's no room for us in any of the inns."

"I'm sorry," the old man sighed. "You would have been welcome to stay here, but a family with children arrived just before you came, and I have taken them in. I don't even have a small corner free now. But try my neighbour. He has a good heart."

"Thank you for your friendliness," Joseph said, and he knocked at the next house.

Here he met with the same answer, and at the house after that, and so on right to the end of the street. Too many people had come to Bethlehem at the command of the mighty Emperor.

"If the donkey could manage it, I think it would be best to go back to the shepherds," Joseph finally decided. "But I don't know if he could find the way in the dark."

"God will help us," Mary said to comfort him. "Be calm, Joseph. The donkey has found somewhere for us to stay every time."

"I hope you are right, Mary," Joseph replied, "but the donkey has changed."

Yes, the donkey was quite different from his usual self. He had severe pain in his leg, and he was very tired. He let his head hang down almost to the ground. That is why he didn't see the angel.

But the angel knew what to do. When the donkey didn't look up, he waved to the birds of Nazareth. They came immediately. They had watched the donkey, Joseph and Mary wandering here and there through Bethlehem all the afternoon, and they were very worried. Now they were happy again! Suddenly the donkey pricked his ears. What sort of birds were these chirping away so loud and clear in the cold and dark?

Of course, they were the birds of Nazareth. And what were they singing?

"Come, come, come, little donkey! Here there is warmth and shelter."

He stretched his neck and lifted up his head. He saw the angel at the end of a side street. Without limping, he stepped out eagerly in his direction.

"Do you hear that, Joseph?" Mary asked in surprise. "My birds are singing."

"I do," Joseph said. "It's strange. I have never heard birds chirping in the middle of the night before, let alone in such a cold one."

"The donkey has found the way," smiled Mary. "He is in a hurry suddenly."

Now the donkey broke into a real trot and Joseph had to run to keep up, which he didn't mind.

The thick clouds that had darkened the sky over Bethlehem all afternoon and evening suddenly vanished at this moment; the sky cleared.

A big star was shining right over the town, a star which no one had seen before. When the donkey rounded the next corner, they approached a house that was gleaming and white. At the door an angel beckoned and smiled, while in the garden the birds of Nazareth were chirping. Joseph and Mary heard the birds singing and saw the house, but they couldn't see the angel.

"What kind of a palace is this?" asked the astonished Joseph. "It is glittering all over. What can it be built with? It must be the house of a very rich man."

"We can't go in there," Mary said anxiously. "Not simple people like us. But Joseph, it feels like the donkey led us here on purpose.

Joseph tried to hold the donkey back, but the donkey was very stubborn.

"Joseph dear," said Mary, "perhaps it's all right after all. My birds are singing in the garden."

"Are they really?" Joseph asked in astonishment.

But when the came nearer to the house, Joseph and Mary saw that it wasn't wealthy and big at all, as they had first thought. It was a plain old stable with twisty walls. The radiant starlight had made it appear brilliantly white and splendid.

"Oh!" Mary cried in delight. "Only a stable! This is where we're supposed to stay all right. I would never have expected to stay in some fine house. We are much too dirty and covered with dust."

"Good," said Joseph and heaved a sigh of relief. "We'll stay here. That suits me. I'll ask the old man at the door."

There really was an old, stooping man standing in front of the house. He had heard the unusual bird song in the dark night, and had gone out to look at these birds. Then he noticed the star with its bright light. But because he was standing in front of the stable he didn't notice that the star was making it shine like silver. He saw the donkey coming along the road with Mary and Joseph. The light of the star fell on them with such brilliance that the old man believed that a king and queen were approaching him.

"There comes the king I have dreamed about," he thought. "And his queen is with him too. What beautiful clothes they are wearing, as if they were woven from silver threads. And whoever saw such a donkey! He is as glossy as the finest silk and his hoofs gleam like pure gold. How can I find the courage to ask them into my house?"

The old man began to tremble with excitement as the travellers drew near. But these people were poor. A quite ordinary donkey was carrying a poor young woman on his back, and the man who was leading the donkey had simple and dusty clothes.

While the old man was standing and blinking in astonishment, Joseph bowed deeply and said: "Good friend, please give us shelter for tonight. We are all very tired. My wife and the donkey must rest."

The old man opened the door. "I only have this old stable. There is enough room in it along with my two sheep and my cow. If you're happy with that."

"Of course we'll be happy," Joseph said. "Nothing would please us more."

"It's strange," the old man told them. "Last night in a dream I was ordered to clean and tidy my stable and to bring all my hay in from the field, because a king would come to visit. And when I woke up, I carried all these orders out, although I laughed at myself for doing so. What would a king want with my stable? What would he want hay for? And then you came along the road, and everything gleamed so brilliantly, as though you really were King Solomon and the Queen of Sheba. In fact, you are poor travellers. I prefer that; I would have been shy before a king. But I am standing here talking. Come in!"

"Do you know, old man," said Mary, "at first we thought that your house was a shining palace. But then we realised that the bright star had made it look like silver."

"A remarkable evening," the old man said. "This great star, which has not been seen before, and bird song in the middle of a winter's night. This is what made me come outside."

"Those are my birds," Mary explained. "They have flown after us all the way from Nazareth. I'm sure they were calling the donkey, to help us find our way."

"God's ways are strange," the old man said. "Would you like to share my simple supper and then rest? What a good thing that I brought all my hay home today. You will be able to lie on it."

"We are really comfortable here," Mary said.

"No king and no queen could have anything better," Joseph laughed.

But the little donkey was already asleep in a corner.

He had carried Mary to her destination. At last he could rest.

The child

The little donkey was dreaming. He dreamed that he was back home in Nazareth and grazing in Mary's meadow. It was early in springtime and all around everything was in blossom and green and fragrant. The birds were singing and flying here and there in sheer delight. He heard someone crying and suddenly knew that the birds were celebrating Mary's child. His heart thumped with joy. "The baby is born now," thought the donkey in his dream.

Even the sun wanted to do something, and shone so dazzlingly bright in his eyes that it woke him up. "Oh, it was only a dream," thought the disappointed donkey.

It wasn't spring, and not even Nazareth, but the old, tumbledown stable in Bethlehem.

But – there was the scent of spring flowers – and there was singing – and everything was dazzlingly bright. The donkey opened his eyes and looked around him.

In a corner of the stable Mary was sitting and in a circle around her was a group of angels, and they were singing.

The angels pressed closer and closer to Mary and even touched her with their wings. What were they trying to see? A warm feeling came over the donkey.

Suddenly an angel moved a little to one side and the donkey had a clear view. Oh! Mary was holding a tiny baby!

He really had been born!

Joseph had opened the baggage and spread out the lovely baby clothes and blankets Mary had sewn. The angels passed them to Mary and Mary wrapped the baby up fine and warm in them. Then she lifted the little one up so they could all see him, and then handed him to Joseph. Joseph put him down

on the hay in a manger, the animals' feeding trough. Then all
the angels stood round the manger and sang. They sang very
beautifully and so softly that they could hardly be heard.

Joseph and the owner of the stable listened peacefully to the
angels and gazed at the child. By chance Mary looked towards
the donkey and noticed how he was craning his neck.

"Oh, Joseph," she said, "show him to our little donkey."

Joseph led the donkey to the manger. There the donkey
smelled the fragrance of spring flowers in the hay.

Suddenly it was dark in the stable. The angels had all
disappeared.

But through a gap in the roof the radiant star shone down right onto the manger while everything else was in darkness. The donkey saw quite clearly how there was radiant light around the baby. Joseph and the old man saw it too.

"The star's light is so bright," the old man said, "that it places the child on a throne. Now I begin to understand why I dreamed that a king would come here."

The little child lay there with his large, dark eyes open. The donkey tried to sniff and smell him a little. What lovely cheeks he had, how warm and soft they were! He had eyes like an angel.

The old man said, "Mary, look how bright your baby's eyes are! Like bright stars! You could believe that the glory of the kingdom of heaven is reflected in them. What kind of child can this be?"

He was soon to hear the answer.

There was a knock at the door. The old man opened it. Outside were the shepherds that Joseph and Mary had rested with the previous night. The donkey immediately recognised Reuben.

"Is there a newly born child here?" a shepherd asked.

"A child wrapped in blankets and lying in a manger?" cried a clear, eager voice.

"Yes," replied the old man. "Come in. But please be quiet."

The shepherds walked across the stable and approached the manger on tiptoe.

In front of the manger they fell to their knees. For a long while, they didn't move. Reuben's eyes were very bright and his old grandfather was wiping tears away. The donkey heard angels singing outside.

The shepherds stood up again slowly and hesitantly, as though they would gladly have kneeled and prayed longer.

"Where are the child's parents?" the grandfather asked. "We have a wonderful story to tell them."

When the shepherds saw Joseph and Mary they were very surprised.

"It's you?" they said. "We expected to find rich people. But God knows best."

Then the old shepherd began to tell their story. "We were keeping watch over our flocks as usual. The night was strangely clear because of the light from a big star we hadn't seen before. Suddenly an angel of the Lord appeared to us, and we were filled with fear. And the angel said to us: 'Do not be afraid. I bring you good news of great joy that will be for all the people. Today in the town of David a Saviour has been born to you; he is Christ the Lord. And this will be a sign for you: you will find a child wrapped in cloths and lying in a manger.'

"And suddenly we saw all the sky was full of angels singing: 'Glory to God in the highest, and on earth, peace to those on whom his favour rests'.

"Then the angels went away and we said to one another, 'Let's go to Bethlehem and see this thing that has happened, which the Lord has told us about.' Hurriedly we set out."

"But how did you find your way here?" asked the old man, puzzled.

"That wasn't difficult," a shepherd answered. "At first we went along the usual road to Bethlehem. Then we saw the star shining over this house while all the others were in darkness. We knew that it was the glory of God being poured over the house."

"My stable!" the old man said.

For some time it was quiet then. The shepherds stood and gazed at the child. It was difficult for them to tear themselves away.

"If only I could stay with you and the little child," Reuben sighed as he stroked the little donkey.

"So I did learn what sort of a child this is," the old man reflected. "Just think! The Saviour in my stable!"

"The Good Shepherd," Reuben said, smiling happily.

"Truly, God has given us great joy," his grandfather said. "Now we must go back to our flocks. It is time to drive the animals out to pasture."

The shepherds left. Day began to break. The star grew pale. The little child, Mary and Joseph were asleep. But the donkey continued to stand by the manger. Joseph had forgotten to lead him back to his stall. He stood quite still, guarding the little child.

He thought of his friends back home in Nazareth. The donkey knew that it would be quite a long time before Mary could travel home with the child. Joseph had said so the day before. Too many people had come to Bethlehem to have their names written down.

With all his heart, the donkey wanted the animals at home to hear about the child.

"What a pity," he thought. "Here is the most lovely child in the world. He has eyes which reflect the glory of God. And the sheep, the goats and their young ones don't know. They are all waiting so impatiently. How can I send a message?"

While the donkey stood and racked his brains, the sun rose. The birds of Nazareth in the trees round the stable woke up and began to sing their song of celebration. One of them peeped through a hole in the roof.

"Donkey!" he whispered. "Can we see the child? We saw and heard the angels in the night and knew that the baby had been born. But we didn't dare sing with the angels. Can we come in now?"

Already a sparrow had flown through the hole. It was the little bird who always hopped sideways. He perched quickly on the edge of the manger.

"Shh!" hissed the donkey.

But when the bird saw the child he just couldn't keep still. He gave a tiny "Peep." This was too much for his comrades outside. They pushed through the hole in the roof and soon the whole flock was in the stable. They perched wherever they could find room, close, very close to the manger! One or two even perched on the sleeping Mary, and a whole crowd of them on the donkey.

"Shh! You must be quiet! Shh!" the donkey warned them. "You can look, but you must keep still or you'll wake him."

For a moment the birds really were as quiet as mice. When the boldest of them couldn't wait any longer and perched on the baby's hand, three others hurriedly flew across and chased him away.

"You must behave," whispered the donkey. "Otherwise you can't stay here." Now the child moved his tiny hand in his sleep. This was too much for the birds. They sang their song of celebration again. They trilled and chirped and sang!

Mary woke up and smiled, and then Joseph woke up too. He had to laugh.

The old man said that nothing could ever surprise him after this.

Finally the baby woke up too. The birds were silent now, ashamed and anxious because they had woken him. Only the boldest bird dared to fly down onto the manger and show off his skill.

"My little birds," Mary said. "Thank you for your song. Now you have seen my child. I think the best thing now would be for you to fly back home. I am sure it's very quiet in Nazareth without you."

Now the little donkey realised how he could send a message.

"My dear birds," he said. "Do what Mary says and fly home. And tell everyone – especially the lambs and the little goats – what has happened here."

"We still want to sing a cradle song for the little child," they begged. "Can we?"

And they sang so beautifully and so softly that the little boy closed his eyes again and went back to sleep.

Then the birds flew away, through the hole in the roof. They chirped goodbye and disappeared, heading north towards Nazareth.

"How lucky you are, being able to go home," the donkey thought. "I am homesick for Nazareth too. All the same, I am luckier than all the others, because I can stay with the child and with Mary and Joseph, and be their little donkey."

Bethlehem

Mary's little donkey was tethered outside the old stable.

"We've been here in Bethlehem a long time now," he was thinking as he munched some fresh hay. "I'm longing to get back home to Nazareth. I can just imagine how Mary's lambs and goats are waiting for us. 'Are they coming soon, Mother?' they'll be crying, and stamping their feet impatiently." The donkey laughed to himself as he thought of his little playmates at home. "But soon we'll be going. I heard Joseph saying to Mary today: 'There are only a few families left to be enrolled,' and Mary said: 'Dear Joseph, why are we the last?' Then Joseph answered: 'They all say they are in a hurry,' and Mary sighed: 'Of course we are well housed here, but I do long for our own little home. I'm always thinking of our animals back there.' – 'Don't fret, Mary,' said Joseph, 'in a couple of days we'll be on our way home.'"

And the little donkey gave a happy little hee-haw.

He said it cautiously in case Mary's baby was asleep in the stable. He didn't want to wake him. And that made him think of the baby: "He is so soft and tender. And his eyes shine just like the good spring sunshine after the long winter, and no other child in all the world has eyes like his. That's what all the shepherds said. And the old man in the stable too. And his black cow and the nice kind sheep think so too."

And when the donkey thought about the child he had to say "Hee-haw" again.

"What are you laughing about, little donkey?" asked the sheep who was eating the bit of grass by the stable wall.

"Oh, I'm just thinking about Mary's baby," said the donkey.

"He's the loveliest baby in all the world, and the nicest and cleverest and sweetest and ..."

"Rarest and finest," added the sheep, who didn't think the donkey was overdoing it. "Have you ever thought how lovely it sounds when the baby laughs?"

"Yes, I think it sounds just like angels singing! Remember how they sang the night he was born."

The sheep turned the idea over in her mind. "Mm, perhaps you're right, but I think it sounds more like when it's raining."

"When it's raining!" cried the donkey, astonished.

"Yes, when the rain drops tinkle into the rain barrel. Or like little bells."

"Angels singing," said the donkey firmly.

The black cow, who was taking a nap, opened her eyes and said: "A little while ago I heard Mary saying to my master that you would be going home soon. Is that true, little donkey?"

"Yes, definitely," replied the donkey, flicking his tail happily.

"Can't you stay a bit longer?" begged the sheep. "Until the baby can walk? It would be such fun to see him running about. Or wait at least until he can crawl."

"No, that's impossible," explained the donkey. "Mary has her animals who are waiting, and Joseph has his work."

"I really wanted to hear the boy talk," sighed the cow. "I'm sure he will only learn gentle and good words."

"Yes, I'm sure of that," agreed the donkey.

"Can't you stay until he begins to talk?" asked the cow. "That's not so long is it?"

"No," answered the donkey. "We're leaving this week."

The cow and the sheep were sad, but the donkey lifted up his head happily and looked at the sky.

"Oh look! What a beautiful star!" he said. The other two looked up. The sun had just set and the darkness was sweeping in. The great star shone more and more clearly.

"Ah ha," said the donkey, "now I recognise it: it's the same star that shone over the stable when we came here. It shone just as clear and bright that night when the baby was born."

"I wonder what's going to happen tonight," the sheep murmured. "Perhaps the angels are coming here again."

"Who knows!" said the cow.

The strangers

Mary and Joseph went outside.

"How wonderful it is tonight," said Mary. "So quiet. And so light."

"As if it was some festival," added Joseph.

The old man stuck his head out. "Hey, what's that shining there?" he asked.

"I recognise it now," cried Mary in some surprise. "It's the same star that brought us here the night the baby was born. Oh, I wonder what's going to happen tonight."

"Oh yes, that was the night you arrived," recalled the old man. "Over there at the bend in the road I saw you, and I thought it was a king and queen coming."

"And it was only us poor folk. But look, there *is* someone coming!" said Mary.

"Tonight it really is grand folk who are travelling," exclaimed Joseph, amazed. "Look what huge camels they have. They're shining like silver."

"And what noble riders they are!" cried Mary. "Joseph, they're coming here!"

"Nothing can surprise me any more," said the stable man.

The travellers came up to the stable, and now you could see clearly how grand they were. Their camels were very, very beautiful and they had saddles and bridles studded with gold and precious stones which shone and sparkled in the starlight when the first camel shook its head.

And what fine riders they were. In their rich clothes they looked like princes.

"We are seeking the newborn King of the Jews," said the first.

"We have seen his star in the East, and it has led us to this house," said the second.

"We have come to worship the Light of the World," said the third.

Joseph was so surprised he couldn't speak. He looked round for Mary, but she had gone inside to the child.

The three travellers were still quite sure that they had come to the right place, because they beckoned to their servants to help them dismount.

Now Joseph noticed that there were several smaller camels behind the three bigger ones. Riders jumped quickly from their saddles and hurried forward to help their lords.

The first stranger was tall and stately. He stretched out his arms towards the star. Then he looked like a giant, thought Joseph – like a young champion.

"Now," the stranger asked in his deep voice, "Where is the Child-King?"

Joseph didn't know what to answer, but just then a happy baby sound came from inside the stable.

"In there!" cried the second traveller. He was not as stately as his tall friend. But he had sharp eyes and such an air of authority that Joseph guessed he was a man who ruled over many people. Still, even he had to bend his proud neck when he entered the stable.

The third stranger, however, had to be lifted down from his camel. He was very old and thin and bent, and he leaned heavily on his stick when he walked.

It was dark in the stable, but through a gap in the roof the starlight shone on to the crib, and it gleamed and glimmered all round the baby lying on the straw, smiling at the newcomers.

"Is it the star that is shining like that, or does the light come from the child?" the strangers wondered, as they bowed to the ground in front of the little one. Then the baby began to gurgle contentedly, filling the little stable with his happy sound so that even the dignified lords had to smile.

The strong warrior bent his knee. The baby started to struggle as hard as he could to reach him. Mary lifted up the child and laid him in the strong man's arms.

"O you, king of all the earth," whispered the man, "I am the strongest of men, but I am as weak as a baby when I hold you in my arms, because you are stronger than me."

Humbly he kissed the little fingers and handed the baby to the second traveller, the proud ruler with the sharp eyes.

"Oh, now I can hold you in my arms," said he softly. "You who will be ruler of all the world. I am rich and mighty, and men obey every wave of my hand, but compared to you I am poor and unimportant, because you are more powerful than me."

Very carefully he kissed the boy's hair and laid him in the arms of the third man, the old stranger who trembled so much he could hardly hold the baby, yet allowed no one to help him.

"Child, child," he whispered, "You have come at last, you for whom the world has waited so long. I possess all wisdom and knowledge but when I hold you in my arms, I admit that I know less than a child, because you are wiser than me."

The baby laughed and tugged hard at the old man's long white beard. Mary hurried forward and unclasped the strong little fingers. The old man kissed the child's forehead and smiled. Then he brought out a soft leather pouch and poured some coarse brown grains into a bowl. He lit them with an ember from the fire and the small stable was filled with billowing fragrant smoke.

Joseph and Mary watched him in wonder. Then he spoke: "We three have come a long way from the lands of the Orient to worship a king. Now we are burning incense in his honour, following the custom of our country."

The princely stranger opened a casket and took out ashes with myrrh, which also had a wonderful scent. But he didn't have to light the myrrh because it was fragrant already.

"The most precious thing I possess is myrrh," he said. "That is what we give to kings in our country."

The young and stately warrior stood by the crib and played with the child, who touched his priceless ring and tried to grab hold of the enormous shining pearl. The man took off his ring and put it in the child's hand.

"Royal Child," said he, "you shall have the ring of truth, because it is the most precious thing that I have."

He brought out gold coins and offered them to Joseph. "Here is gold for the baby," he said.

"Such a little child should not receive such great gifts," protested Mary.

But the old stranger said, "We saw his star when it first shone, one night some months ago. We knew then that at that hour, a great king was born, and we decided to make the journey to find him."

And the younger went on: "We have truly come to worship a king, because the angels said it would happen."

Then the strangers wanted to hear more. Mary told them how the angel Gabriel had come to her in Nazareth and told her that she would have a baby who would be the world's Saviour and King.

They all listened in silence. Then the old man said, "The ways of God are wonderful."

"He has brought us here in a wonderful way," said the two others.

Meanwhile the servants were crowding into the doorway. They were curious about the child who had inspired their masters to come all the way to the Land of Judah. They craned their necks to catch a glimpse of him.

Mary noticed them. "Come in, come in," she said, making room for them round the crib.

"But what is it that is shining so brightly?" whispered the servants. "Is the light coming from the child's eyes, or is it the star shining in?"

"This baby shall be King of the World," said the old man.

The servants fell to their knees and touched the ground with their foreheads. The child smiled just as happily to them as to their royal masters.

"May you always be as gentle as you are now," said one of the servants. "You shall rule the earth with the sceptre of goodness and it will be good to live in your kingdom, even as poor servants."

The baby nodded his head and looked very serious for a moment.

"It's as if he understands," said the servant, amazed.

Mary took the child and laid him in the servant's arms.

"Yes, he will become a king," she said softly. "But he will also be the world's Saviour and then he will be everyone's servant, even the servant of servants."

"O king of kings who shall be the servant of servants," whispered the servant. "God is so good to send you to poor people on earth!"

Mary laid the baby in the crib and he went to sleep at once. The others stood looking at him in silence for a while, the grand lords and the poor servants. Then the stately stranger spoke: "Set up the tents for the night. It is time to rest. Early tomorrow morning we must start on our journey back."

"The journey has taken a long time," he told Joseph later, "and on our return we have to visit King Herod in Jerusalem. On our way here we went to his palace to ask about the newborn King of the Jews. But King Herod had not even heard about him. He was very happy when we told him. And he asked us to return and tell him where the child is, because he, too, wants to come and worship him."

A cold gust of wind blew through the night and the light of the star shone down. Mary shivered and wrapped her shawl round the child. She knew, and Joseph knew, and their host knew, that Herod was a very wicked king and they couldn't believe that he had kind thoughts towards the baby. But they didn't dare say that to their noble guests.

"Joseph, I am so uneasy," whispered Mary after the strangers had gone to their tents. "I'm afraid of King Herod. What if he came here?"

"We must try and get away from here as soon as possible," answered Joseph. "Bethlehem is too close to Jerusalem. We'll be safer at home in Nazareth. I'll be ready tomorrow or the day after, I'm sure, and then we'll be off."

"I really wish that the good men wouldn't tell King Herod where the child is," said Mary. "Can't we ask them not to, Joseph?"

"I'm not sure I would dare speak to such grand folk," replied Joseph uneasily.

"Dear Joseph, you must... for the child's sake," begged Mary.

"Yes, alright, I'll try tomorrow before we set off," Joseph promised.

***

The camels were lying outside the stable. The donkey was tethered to the door. The spring night was mild and smelled beautifully of fresh grass and flowers.

"Little donkey," said one of the camels, "why do your grand owners live in such a tumbledown old stable?"

"Joseph is a poor man," answered the donkey. "He's not grand at all."

"Where does he keep his flocks and herds?" asked another camel.

"Flocks and herds!" cried the donkey. "*I'm* his flocks and herds, that's all he has. Of course at home in Nazareth Mary has a few sheep and goats."

"Do you mean to say that it's a poor man that you work for?" puzzled the camel. "Why then have our rich masters come all the way here to visit him?"

"That I don't know," replied the donkey. "But would I be any happier with a master rich in money? Mary and Joseph are rich in goodness and kindness and helpfulness. It is wonderful to have a master who never beats me or shouts or wants to make me carry more than I can manage."

"You're right there," agreed the camel, "We animals appreciate a good man more than a rich one. But tell me, little donkey, what's so special about the child in there? I heard our masters talking about him during the journey. They've hardly spoken about anything else. Who is he?"

"He is the Good Shepherd," said the donkey quietly.

"The Good Shepherd!" cried the camel.

"The Good Shepherd!" echoed the other animals. "Is that true?"

"The angels sang about him all night long when he was born. He is the Saviour of the whole world, and its King and Shepherd," said the donkey proudly.

Then the camels lifted up their heads to the clear spring sky. For the rest of the night they were silent, thinking over what they'd been told. When at last day was breaking, the donkey spoke: "On your way home, if you pass through a town called Nazareth please will you say hello to all the animals there, and tell them that all's well with the child and Mary and Joseph. And tell them we're coming home soon."

"We've never heard of such a town," answered the camels, "but if we do go that way, we won't forget. But now we have a request to make to you."

"What is it?" asked the donkey.

"We want to see the child before we go home. Can you help us?"

"I'll try," the donkey promised.

In the morning, as they were coming out of their tents, the tall warrior said: "Last night I dreamed that an angel came and commanded me to go back home another way, and not to go to Jerusalem to speak with the king."

"Strange!" cried his companion. "That is exactly what I dreamed too."

At that moment the old stranger came slowly towards them. "I was told by angels in a dream that we should return using another route," he said.

"That's what we dreamed too! We should obey."

So they decided to go straight home. Joseph was pleased when he heard that.

"It was God who sent the dreams to the strangers," he thought. "He knows how shy I am. He saw that I didn't dare to speak to them. That was good of him!"

"Now perhaps you will travel through Nazareth," said the donkey to the camels, "and say hello to the animals there."

"We'll do that for you," said the camels, "but you must keep your promise too."

Then the donkey started to bray and scrape the door with his hoof until Mary came out.

"Wait a bit, my little donkey," she said. "I'll come and give you your water soon."

And she went in again.

"Oh dear," said the camel, disappointed.

"Wait a bit," said the donkey cheerfully. "She hasn't got the baby up yet."

The animals waited impatiently while the servants saddled them, and then they heard the baby wake up inside the stable.

"Now!" said the donkey, and he brayed and pawed the ground until at last Mary came out. She had the child in her arms.

"Ooh!" said all the camels.

The servants completely forgot themselves as they came to look at the little one.

"What's the matter with you today?" Mary asked her donkey.

But he kept on shaking his head and pawing the ground, so Mary went up to him.

"Are you ill?" she wondered. "You don't usually make all this fuss!"

The donkey laid his head on Mary's shoulder.

"Oh, you just want to say good morning, you little rascal," said Mary, laughing. "Well, you can do that."

The camels craned their heads forward to her, and she lifted up the child quite close to them before she went in again.

"You did that well, little donkey," said the camels, "so thank you very much. We'll never forget that you let us see the Good Shepherd."

The dream

The little donkey woke up with a start. His heart was beating and he was strangely frightened. At the same time, he heard the child stir in the crib.

"Ah, there he is after all," he thought thankfully. "Everything's okay. It was just a dream. It's terrible what you can dream."

And what a dream he had had! He had dreamed that they had come home to Nazareth and all Mary's animals had come rushing up to welcome them:

"Can we see the child? Can we see the baby?" cried all the little goats and lambs, skipping with excitement. "Where is the child?"

It was then that the donkey noticed that the child was not with them. Nor was Mary. Nobody was riding on his back, only a big heavy bundle.

"What have you done with the child?" asked the oldest sheep.

"He was there just a minute ago," puzzled the donkey.

"But where is he now, and where's Mary?"

Indeed where was the baby, and where was Mary? The donkey was very worried.

"Maybe you left them in the wilderness and a lion has eaten them up?" asked the goats.

"Did they slip off your back over the cliffs and on to the rocks below?" suggested the sheep.

"Did you lose them in the river when you crossed it?" cried the lambs.

But the donkey couldn't remember anything like that. Only that he had been hurrying up the hill to Nazareth to show the child to his friends.

"And we've been so longing to see him," wailed the little lambs and the goats.

The donkey felt his heart tighten with fear. It was then that he had woken up and found it was only a dream, and he was standing in the dark in the stable in Bethlehem; Mary, Joseph and the old man were asleep on the straw on the floor, and the child was lying in the crib.

"*We've been so longing...*" heard the donkey, like an echo from his dream.

"That was because Joseph and Mary were talking so much about the journey home yesterday evening," he thought.

Joseph had said that everything was done now and they could go home.

"I've been so longing for this," said Mary. "We've been here nearly three months now, and the baby's getting quite big."

"Yes, he'll manage the journey home fine," said Joseph.

"And the spring sunshine is bright and warm. Everything is so beautiful you could think you were walking in God's meadows in paradise," said Mary. "Dear Joseph, what a lovely journey home it will be!"

"Yes, it'll be quite different from when we were coming here. It was winter then and cold. It rained so much! Do you remember?"

"But our good donkey helped us," said Mary. "Think how much it will mean to him to be going home. I've seen how homesick he is."

That was how they had been talking before they went to sleep, and it had made the donkey so happy. And then he had a horrible dream.

"But a dream is only a dream and it doesn't mean anything," he thought.

Just then he noticed that it was growing light in the stable. There was a faint gleam, which gradually grew brighter. At last the donkey could clearly make out an angel in shining robes. The angel bent down over Joseph and whispered: "Joseph, Joseph, listen carefully!"

But Joseph turned in his sleep and thrashed out with his arms as if he wanted to chase away the angel that was disturbing his sleep.

"Joseph," said the angel, "get up at once. Wake up Mary. Gather together everything you have. Take the child and run, but don't go home. King Herod wants to kill the child, and you have to hide in Egypt for a while. Don't be afraid; the angels will protect you. Listen Joseph, wake up now! There is no time to lose!"

Joseph stirred, mumbled and opened his eyes.

The angel stroked the donkey's nose and it was like the softest breath of the west wind.

"Mary's little donkey," whispered the angel, "you must help me to take the child somewhere safe."

Then the angel vanished.

"What did I just dream?" wondered Joseph. "That I should

run away to Egypt with the child! What an idea! No, no, tomorrow we're all set to go home to Nazareth. That'll be good." Joseph wanted to snuggle down and sleep again.

But the donkey stamped and neighed so that Joseph woke fully and got up.

"What's the matter?" he asked.

The donkey brayed so that it echoed through the little stable. He made it sound very urgent. Mary woke up, and the old man woke up.

"What is it?" asked Mary. "I'm so afraid, but what is the danger?"

"It was only the donkey that frightened you. Lie down and sleep a bit longer."

"No," said Mary, "something's wrong. He doesn't bray like that for nothing."

"Well," said Joseph thoughtfully, "I did have a strange dream. An angel came to me and said we should travel to Egypt at once and stay there for a while because King Herod wants to kill our child."

"Oh!" said Mary shivering, "I am so afraid of him. We must run away. At once. Now, in the night."

"But Mary, it was only a dream. Sleep now. Tomorrow we can think it over."

But the donkey brayed again.

"No," said Mary, "I believe that the donkey has seen the angel and knows he really did speak to you. You can see from the donkey's fear that there is real danger. Let's leave at once, Joseph."

Then Joseph realised that the angel really had warned him in the dream. He quickly helped Mary to pack and load up the donkey. It was still dark but he fanned the embers on the hearth so that they could see.

The old man who looked after the stable was sad.

"Do you have to go so soon?" he asked. "Right in the middle of the night! Wait until morning at least."

"We have to hurry," said Joseph. "The baby is in danger."

87

"Oh, no one's going to harm a little child! It's just a bad dream you've had."

"But the angel I saw in my dream told me to leave at once," answered Joseph firmly, "and our donkey also saw the angel."

"At least wait until it gets light," begged the old man. "There are still some wild animals about, and they could kill you and the baby."

"We're not afraid of wild animals," said Joseph. "It's not them that are after the child's life."

"Who is it then?" asked the old man.

"King Herod!"

"Yes, but the strangers from the East didn't go to see him on their way back after all. He can't know yet where the baby is," objected the old man.

"Somehow he's found out," said Joseph. "And he wants to kill the child because he can't bear that goodness and justice should have any power here on earth."

"Well, do as you think best," said the old man, "and may the Lord preserve you."

"We are very grateful to you for letting us stay here in your stable all this time," said Joseph. "See here is a yoke I've made for you from an olive root I found in a crevice."

"That *is* well made," said the old man, "Thank you very much. My old yoke was falling to bits and couldn't be mended."

"Yes, I saw you needed a new one," said Joseph smiling.

Mary took the old man's hand and said, "Here, I have sewn a cloak for you from cloth I got from the men of the East."

"Oh, it's so warm and soft! It's much too fine for me, but I *do* like it. My cloak is getting a bit worn out."

"I saw that you needed one," said Mary. "Isn't it lucky I got it ready in time?"

"Now that you're going," said the man, "I'd like to thank you for honouring my poor stable by coming here so that the Saviour of the World was born in it. No place on earth is as great and holy as this little hut."

By now the donkey was getting restless. How much longer

were they going to stand around saying goodbye? Hadn't the angel said there was no time to lose? He pawed the ground and butted Joseph in the back.

"Yes, yes," said Joseph, "we must hurry."

Mary went into the stable. The child was still sleeping in the crib and smiled in his sleep as Mary lifted him up.

Mary wrapped the baby in a shawl and handed him to the old man who carried him out to the donkey. Joseph lifted Mary on to the donkey's back. The old man kissed the child's cheek and handed him back to his mother. They set off.

***

The donkey trotted at full speed. Joseph had to run to keep up with him.

It was still dark, but the donkey could see quite well in the dark and soon found a little path that led out on to the high road.

"It's just as well," said Mary thoughtfully, "that we didn't get a room at one of the inns inside the walls. We wouldn't have been able to get out of the town before the gates were opened in the morning. And maybe even then, it would have been too late."

"Yes, it was good that we were staying out here," said Joseph. "Now the roads are open." Suddenly he called out:

"Wait! My cloak is caught in a bush."

Mary reined in the donkey while Joseph freed himself.

"It's so quiet," said Mary. "Look, it's growing light in the east. Soon the sun will be up."

The donkey pricked up his ears. He had heard hoof beats far off.

Now Joseph could hear them too.

"It's horsemen," he said. "Who could be out so early?"

The hoof beats came nearer and nearer.

"Let's hide in the wood over there," said Joseph, taking hold of the donkey's bridle.

No sooner were they in the wood than a troop of soldiers rode by in a great hurry without seeing Joseph and Mary. Just as they reached the top of a hill in the direction of Bethlehem, the sun rose and its first rays gleamed on their polished helmets.

89

"Oh," breathed Mary, "I'm glad we hid out of their way."

"Yes indeed," said Joseph. "But now we should hurry on."

Neither Joseph nor Mary had any idea that the soldiers had been sent by King Herod to look for their child.

All day they travelled south, not daring to stop and rest. Towards evening they were very tired. The sun went down and it grew dark.

"It's quite eerie in the wilderness tonight," said Mary.

"We'll have to stay here all the same," said Joseph.

Mary slid down from the donkey. They ate some bread which the old man in the stable had given them, and the donkey chewed some hay which he had carried on his back.

Joseph and Mary lay down on the ground with their heads against the donkey's belly. The child stretched his hands towards the sky as if to play with the gleaming lights up there.

Suddenly there was a shooting star, and he cried out happily as it shot through space.

"The baby isn't afraid of the dark," said Joseph. "He feels just as safe out here as in the stable."

"Look how he reaches up with his arms to the stars," said Mary. "Look how they twinkle to him as if they were good friends."

Joseph and Mary became so interested in the child's play that they forgot their fears and worries. The donkey began to snore softly and soon the baby fell asleep too. Even Joseph and Mary slept peacefully until it began to grow light again.

With the caravan

All the next day the little donkey trotted southwards carrying Mary and the child on his back. Joseph walked silently beside them.

There were fewer and fewer olive groves and vineyards now, and homes became more and more scattered, until finally they came to an end altogether. The country stretched out ahead of the travellers, bare and empty. The sun blazed down, scorching hot. They had reached the huge desert that separates the Land of Judah from Egypt. The donkey got very tired from wading through the desert sands, and the fine dust got into his eyes and nostrils. But it was not only the donkey who found the going difficult; the sand was bothering Joseph and Mary too. Only the little child, who was asleep most of the time, well wrapped up in his mother's shawl, was untroubled.

"I'm so thirsty!" thought the donkey. "I've never been so thirsty. But if I push on hard, perhaps we'll reach Egypt tonight." And so he tried to take bigger steps in the deep sand.

Mary was looking forward to getting there too, because in the early afternoon she said:

"Joseph, do you think we'll get there today?"

But Joseph shook his head and said, "Dear Mary, everyone says it's a long way to Egypt. Many days' journey, I think. But don't worry, the angel promised to help us."

Mary sat silent for a while, but suddenly she called out: "I can see buildings over there! And trees! It's the beginning of Egypt. Can't you see? Over there!"

Yes, far, far away they could just see houses and some trees. The little donkey quickened his steps, quite excited. Wonderful! They'd be there soon.

But it was only a stopping place for travellers at an oasis, somewhere to stay overnight. The travellers often had lots of camels, carrying goods through the desert from one place to another. These groups of camels were known as 'caravans'.

A large caravan had just arrived at the stopping place. A rich merchant had hired a whole caravan of camels and camel drivers to carry his goods through the desert. As Joseph and Mary entered the inn, the merchant himself was sitting at a table, and the man who owned the inn stood beside him, chatting.

"It's not hard for you to travel through the desert, with all your money and your camels," said the innkeeper. "But every day I see single families going by as well. They're running away from King Herod, but most of them end up lost in the sand, and are never seen again. They're usually very tired by the time they arrive here, and they've hardly covered any desert yet!"

Joseph and Mary looked at each other in alarm. Now they knew that their journey was going to be very difficult indeed.

"The angel will protect us," whispered Joseph and squeezed Mary's hand.

Then the innkeeper noticed them.

"What do you want?" he asked roughly.

"Sir, can we and our donkey stay here tonight?" answered Joseph.

"Can you pay?"

Joseph opened his purse and took out one of the pieces of gold that the rich strangers had given to the child. At the same time, the ring fell out by accident and rolled along the floor to the table where the merchant sat. The merchant was going to kick it away but then he saw what a large pearl gleamed in the shadows.

Joseph bent down and picked up the ring.

"What a ring!" thought the merchant. "I've never seen anything like it! I wouldn't have believed such a large pearl even existed!"

"Where did you get that?" he asked, looking hard at Joseph. "You must be a thief. Why are you out here in the desert?"

"The baby was given the ring by a very rich man," said Joseph calmly.

"The baby!" snorted the merchant. "People don't give rings to a baby! Tell me the truth! Where did you steal the ring and the gold coin from?"

"Joseph is telling the truth," said Mary. "The baby was given them both by some rich strangers."

The merchant looked closely at her. What could this mean? The poor woman met his gaze with such clear eyes that it was impossible that she was lying, indeed impossible she was even capable of thinking up a lie. So he peered at the child. There was nothing especially remarkable about the baby as he slept in his mother's arms. Who would give such a tiny bundle expensive presents?

"Hmm," he said, "will you sell the ring?"

"No," said Joseph. "It belongs to the baby and he loves playing with it."

"These folk don't understand how valuable the ring is," thought the merchant. "Good! One way or another, I'll get that ring!"

"Where are you going?" he asked in a rather more friendly tone.

"To Egypt," answered Joseph.

That made the merchant happy. No one could travel through the desert with a little child on just a donkey. So, he would invite these people to travel with his caravan and he would make sure they owed him a lot of money for food and water. Then he would take the ring in payment. Yes, that would work!

"Now just listen," he said, "you can't go travelling through the desert on just a donkey. But I like you, and I like helping people: you can travel with my caravan and then you will arrive safely in Egypt."

Joseph bowed humbly and Mary smiled happily. "You are a very good man, sir," said Joseph.

"God will reward you for being so good," said Mary.

***

"Have you heard anything like this before?" said the leader of the caravan when he came out to his men. "The merchant has allowed those poor folk with the donkey to travel with us to Egypt."

"What has he got in mind?" asked one of the men. "He's not doing that just to help them."

"He's got a heart of stone," said another.

"He has given them permission," said the leader, "and there's nothing we can do about it."

"Did you hear?" said one of the big beautiful camels when they were left alone. "We're going to have a donkey for company through the desert."

"Ugh!" said another, turning up his nose. "That's not the sort of company I want!"

"How will a donkey keep up with us when we really get going?" asked a third.

"He'll collapse before we've got half way," said a fourth.

"That is the best thing that could happen," said the oldest camel. "Then we'll arrive in Egypt without him and we won't need to feel embarrassed."

"Hush!" said the first. "Here he comes."

"Act as if you haven't seen him!" said the oldest. "Don't speak to him, and don't answer if he says anything."

Joseph approached, leading the donkey, and Mary followed right behind with the child.

The merchant came out and said, "You'll have to sell the donkey. You can't take him with you."

"Why not?" asked Mary, taken aback.

"He won't keep up with the camels at the speed they go. But I'm sure the innkeeper will buy him for a good price, and then you can ride on my camels."

"We can't sell our donkey," said Joseph.

"He'll manage all right," said Mary.

"We'll be travelling through the desert for many days," said the merchant. "He'll never do it."

"God has given us the donkey," said Mary. "Without the donkey we would be lost, because he hears what we cannot hear and sees what we cannot see."

The merchant was annoyed. "What nonsense! Now be sensible, and sell him."

"Our donkey can see the good angels," said Joseph, "and he has always led us the right way. We are grateful that you wish to help us, but we cannot part with our donkey."

The merchant saw that he couldn't persuade them and so he went back inside, muttering to himself.

"Don't be afraid, little donkey," said Joseph. "We won't sell you."

"Thank you, my own very special little donkey." Mary stroked his nose tenderly, "Thank you for bringing us to this good place."

By now the baby had woken up. When he saw all those splendid camels he began to wriggle and kick. He chuckled and smiled and stretched out his arms towards them as if he wanted to pat them all. Joseph laughed and lifted him up to the nearest one. That happened to be the oldest camel. The huge animal stayed quite still while the little baby stroked it with his outstretched fingers.

Afterwards Mary went inside with the child. Joseph took the baggage off the donkey's back and followed them in.

"Little donkey," said the oldest camel, who had completely forgotten that they were not going to talk to him. "Who are those people, and who is the child?"

"Oh," said the donkey happily, "he is the one that's going to be the Good Shepherd!"

"The Good Shepherd!" echoed the camel. "You don't mean the one that God promised to send to earth from heaven?"

"The very one!" said the donkey.

"Ah!" said all the animals, "the Good Shepherd."

"When he patted me I felt as if I could have run through the desert for days and nights, jumping and dancing."

"When he smiled," said the one next to him, "I could smell the most wonderful scent, like newly mown hay and fresh flowers."

"The scent still lingers in the air," added another.

"Little donkey," said the old camel, "are you really planning to carry the baby and his mother all through the desert to Egypt? You'll never manage it."

"Oh yes, I will. I've already carried Mary all the way from Nazareth to Bethlehem."

"That's not very far. But it's a very, very long way to Egypt. I could carry him and his mother for you."

"No," said the donkey. "No one else is Mary's little donkey. Only me."

"Mm, but what if you get tired?"

"Well, we'll see," said the donkey. "Maybe you could take them now and again."

"Me too, me too," murmured the others.

"Is it true what your master says, that you have seen the angels?" asked another.

"Yes," replied the donkey, "every time there was any danger on the way an angel helped me. And he has promised to help me again."

"But why are you going to Egypt?" asked the old camel.

"The wicked king wants to kill the child."

This news upset all the animals. They started to bawl and bellow and one of the camel drivers came rushing out to see what was the matter. It took a long time before they were all quiet again.

***

Early next morning there was a lot of bustle in the inn. Everything was ready for the departure, except that the rich merchant was still eating. Joseph had fastened the baggage tightly on to the donkey. Mary had got the baby ready and was playing with him, sitting on the donkey's back. The camels craned their long necks to see him laughing, completely forgetting their usual proud ways.

Suddenly they heard the noise of horses' hooves, and very soon a troop of soldiers appeared, coming closer.

"Mary!" cried Joseph, alarmed. "Soldiers are coming! Perhaps they're looking for us! Where can we hide?"

At once all the camels crowded round the donkey and hid him and Mary from the soldiers' view.

The lead soldier slid quickly off his horse, went inside the inn and called out: "Have you seen a young couple with a baby?"

"Who would go off into the desert with a baby?" said the merchant. "What would they do there?"

"They could try to hide the child."

"Why?"

"The king has found out that a child was born in Bethlehem recently, and it has been said that this child will become king one day. And King Herod wants to put a stop to that."

"Well then, why don't you look in Bethlehem?"

"We've ransacked the whole town. But King Herod heard that a young couple who were living in a stable outside the town disappeared with their little child the very night we got there."

"Bah! A royal child doesn't live in a stable," said the merchant, "and you won't find him out here in the desert! Look in the villages around Bethlehem! But first drink a cup of wine with me, so that I can wish you luck."

The soldier drank all the wine, jumped on his horse, and disappeared with his troop in another direction.

But the merchant now had something to think about as the caravan set off on its long journey into the desert.

"I wonder who the child is," he thought. "Ah well, Herod won't get him now. Not his ring either – that will be mine."

Through the desert

The caravan wound through the desert. First came the leading camel with the head driver, then the merchant on the oldest camel, followed by all the others in a long, long line. Last of all trotted the little donkey with Mary and the baby, and Joseph beside them.

"Just wait," muttered the merchant, "soon the donkey will collapse in the sand. Then they'll be glad of my help."

He told the camel driver at the end of the line not to lose sight of the donkey.

But the proud camels slowed their pace so that the donkey could keep up. The drivers yelled and urged the camels on, but it didn't make any difference: the camels just would not go any faster.

"I think the animals have been bewitched," said the head driver. "What's the matter with them?"

"Make them go faster!" said the merchant. "You promised a quick journey." But really he was quite glad that the little family didn't trail too far behind.

Even so, the donkey couldn't help growing tired. When it was time to set up camp towards evening, he had already dropped a good way behind, though he tried bravely to keep up.

"Poor little donkey," said the leading camel, when he arrived at last. "Are you very tired? We tried to stay at your slower pace so that you could keep up with us."

"Oh," said the donkey, "I'll be all right, as long as I can rest. But we're going such a long way from home, and I miss Nazareth. All my friends are waiting there for us. They must be almost crazy with longing to see the child."

"Little donkey," said the oldest camel, "Egypt is still a long way away. You're going to be travelling for many days with your tail pointing towards Nazareth."

"Oh," said the donkey sadly, "but the angel has told us to go, and I know we have to, because of the wicked king."

The next day the desert was even hotter.

"It feels as if the sun is lying right here on the earth and is burning up every living thing!" sighed the donkey.

Occasionally he got a mouthful of precious water which the merchant sold to Joseph from his huge leather bottle.

During the afternoon, the heat was even worse. Suddenly the donkey saw the angel beckoning him to turn off to the left. The donkey obeyed at once, but gave out a piercing *"Hee-haw!"* to warn the camels that danger was approaching.

"What's the matter?" cried Joseph.

"Better let him do what he wants," said Mary, "He always knows which is the right way. I believe he's seen the angel again."

"What's the matter, little donkey?" cried the leading camel.

"The angel told me to go this way," shouted the donkey.

The lead camel suddenly turned around and cantered back to the donkey. All the others followed. The camel drivers yelled and screamed. The merchant woke up from his dozing.

"What on earth's going on?" he grumbled.

"The camels have all gone mad," answered the head driver. "The donkey brayed and they all turned around, despite their drivers yelling at them. I have never known them to do that before."

"Turn the camels around again," commanded the merchant.

"They won't," came the answer.

The men were completely helpless and had to go where the big animals took them.

The angel led the donkey to a large hollow in the ground, protected by huge blocks of stone. There he told the donkey to stop, and soon all the camels arrived too.

"The angel wants us to stay here," declared the donkey.

"Are you sure you've seen right?" asked the leading camel

mildly. "You must be very tired and it's quite common to see mirages in the desert – to see oases and things like that."

"No," said the donkey, "I really did see the angel."

"What's wrong with you?" barked the merchant at Joseph. "Why did you lead the donkey here?"

"I didn't," said Joseph. "He went by himself; he has seen, I'm sure, the good angel that God has sent to help us to Egypt."

"I think you've all gone quite crazy," snapped the merchant. "You and your donkey and the camels and the drivers that let them do what they want."

Suddenly he gave a shout and pointed ahead. Far away a black cloud could be seen.

"A sandstorm!" he cried. "The Lord be praised for leading us to this hollow where we can take shelter."

Everyone got the camp ready at full speed. They had only just finished when the mighty storm hit them. The sand whipped by and everything went dark.

"If we had carried on out there, our lives would have been in danger," said the merchant. "This storm is the worst I've ever seen, but we're all right in here. We're so lucky!"

"It was the angel of the Lord who led the donkey here," said Mary.

"Yes it must have been," agreed the head driver, "but I don't really understand it."

"It's not that difficult," said Joseph. "God sent his angel to help us. We can't see the angel, but our little donkey can. That's why we can safely follow him wherever he goes."

"Yes," said the head driver, "I've never felt as safe in a storm as I do now with you."

"Nor have we," said the other camel drivers. "Now we understand why you won't sell your donkey."

"And from now on I won't try to make you sell him, either," said the merchant.

After that they all sat silent, listening to the roar of the storm. The only thing that could sometimes be heard above its noise was the happy gurgling of the little baby.

By the morning of the next day, it was quiet again.

"I have a suggestion to make," said the merchant, who didn't want to lose sight of Joseph and the ring. "Why don't you and your wife ride on camels. That will make it easier for the donkey to keep up."

Joseph and Mary spoke together and then Joseph said: "We like your idea, thank you for thinking of us and our little donkey."

The camels began to get excited. Which one of them would carry the child on his back? Then they stood carefully, trying to look very quiet and very holy.

One of the pack camels was chosen, and his load was shared out among the others. Mary sat on the strong animal, and he went striding along majestically through the desert.

"Look," said the driver, "the camel really knows he's carrying something special."

But the donkey trotted gloomily behind. He felt so sad and left out, not having Mary on his back.

"Here am I, going along, and I'm now only an ordinary donkey," he thought. "No longer Mary's special donkey. It's much harder without her weight on my back. I wish I could lay my head on Joseph's shoulder now and again for a bit of comfort. And I can't hear the baby. I can't bear it."

But the pack camel was very proud that evening and never stopped telling the others what the woman had said and how the child had patted him as his mother held his little hand.

The next morning they found that the camel had hurt his foot a little and was limping a bit. They put his loads back on him and another animal was chosen for Mary to ride. And every morning, this happened. Each new camel only managed to carry the child and his mother for one day, and then by morning something had gone wrong with him. The animals thought this was a very fair arrangement, but the drivers were puzzled.

"It seems as if that's how the camels want it," said the head driver, who understood his animals well.

But the donkey grew more and more sad. It had been a long time since he had done anything for Mary. All he had to do now was to trot behind the others. He hung his head miserably.

"You're not coping well with the heat," Joseph said at the end of the day, "even though you're not carrying anything."

But the donkey only turned his head away and wouldn't let Joseph stroke him. When Mary came, though, he couldn't help himself, he just had to rub his nose against her cheek.

"We'll soon be in Egypt," she comforted him. "Then it will be just you and me and the baby again."

Then one day, there was no water left.

"We were held up by the sandstorm," said the head driver, "but with luck we'll reach a well before evening. There's a little oasis a half day's journey from here."

That was the worst day of the whole journey. Everyone was so thirsty. The donkey walked as if in a dream, and his feet felt as heavy as lead. He was wet with sweat and completely covered with dust.

"What does it matter now if I die in the desert?" he thought. "Joseph and Mary can manage just as well without me. I'm only getting in the way."

He collapsed and lay in the hot sand.

"We haven't time to wait for him," said the head driver. "We've got to get to the well before we all die of thirst."

Joseph asked if he could get off his camel.

"I'll reach the well with the donkey," he said. "I can't let him die here."

He went back to the donkey and talked to him and comforted him. At last he succeeded in getting him on to his feet, but they were both tired out and thirsty as they staggered forward.

"Keep going!" said Joseph. "The oasis is over there and you'll be able to drink as much as you want."

But when they got there, there was no water. The storm had blown sand into the well, burying the water deep down.

The men were tired out and bad tempered.

"It's all your fault," said the merchant to Joseph, "yours and your donkey's. It's him who's held us back. Otherwise we would have reached Egypt by now."

"The Lord will help us," said Mary gently and went over to the donkey. She was carrying the baby in her arms.

"I wouldn't mind if he did," grumbled the merchant. "But I can't see it happening."

Mary bent over the donkey, who was lying half dead at her feet. Suddenly the child began to laugh. It sounded like a babbling brook.

"Listen to the child," said the head driver. "Only a baby could laugh now."

"Shut him up!" said the merchant who was fevered from thirst. "Oh, is there no one who can sell me a mug of water for a gold coin," he moaned.

No one answered.

"O my baby," whispered Mary, "stroke our donkey. He'll feel better if you just touch him." She took the child's hand and guided it to the donkey's head. The baby gurgled as if he wanted to speak. He wriggled eagerly. The tired animal opened his heavy eyes and looked at the little one. What was he trying to say? The donkey tried to read the answer in the child's clear eyes.

Wait a moment, what's that? An angel! The donkey stirred and lifted his head, and there stood the angel, beckoning. The donkey heaved himself up and tottered towards him.

"The donkey has seen the angel," whispered Mary. "Praise heaven, now we'll get some water."

"Water!" cried everyone and followed the donkey in a long straggling line. The angel led the donkey a short way out into the desert, to a clear well.

Joseph brought water to Mary.

"No, give it to the merchant first," she said. "He's fainted."

When Joseph brought the fresh water to the man's lips, he woke up.

"What kind of water is that?" he asked, "It's refreshed me straight away."

After that, all the men sat talking long into the night about the miracle that had happened and how they had been rescued thanks to Mary's little donkey.

In Egypt

Mary and Joseph could see a green plain of land spread out in front of them. Far away, they could see a broad gleaming streak of water. The camel drivers said that it was the Nile, Egypt's famous river.

"Very soon now, the ring will be mine," thought the merchant happily. "What a beautiful ring it is. I could hardly hold myself back when I saw the baby playing with it. What a silly toy for a baby!"

But a faint voice whispered in the merchant's heart: "Do you really think it's right to take the ring in payment for the small thing that you have done? Isn't it actually *they* who have helped *you*? What happened with the sandstorm and the well?" But the merchant silenced that voice.

"I'll do more for them," he thought, "I could get Joseph some work in Egypt and find the family a house to live in, then I'll have more than earned the ring. Joseph won't be able to find work here by himself. All the same, it will be sad to part from them," he sighed. "It's funny how I've got to like them: quiet old Joseph, and Mary who's always gentle and happy. And the baby, I wish he was my son! I've never liked anyone as much as him, and I'm even fond of their little donkey. Yes, there's something about them... Sometimes I wonder who they really are. But I'll get them a roof over their heads anyway."

They came to a bigger village. The merchant had a friend there that he often visited. He spoke to him about Joseph.

"Listen," he said to Joseph afterwards. "A friend of mine has a garden here in the village where he grows balsam. It's got a bit wild recently, and he'll employ you to look after it. There's also a little house you can sort out and live in."

Joseph and Mary were of course delighted.

"Are you an angel in disguise?" cried Mary. "Sometimes I've almost thought that!"

The merchant blushed.

"How can we repay you for your kindness?" said Joseph. "What could we give you?"

The merchant swallowed hard and said: "The ring!"

Joseph and Mary looked at each other.

"It belongs to the child," said Joseph. "I don't know if we can give it to you."

The baby was sitting in Mary's lap, playing with the ring. It was as if he understood, because he held it out to the merchant with a happy little laugh.

"Look, he's giving it to you," said Mary. "Take it. But you also need to know what kind of a ring it is, because it's no ordinary gold ring. The child received it from a very wise and wealthy man, who said: 'This is the ring of truth. If someone who is kind and good wears the ring, it will shine beautifully. But if someone who is a deceiver and a cheat wears the ring, the pearl won't shine any more.' But you are a good man, and you can wear the ring."

The merchant stood there with the ring in his hand, but – poor man! – now he owned this valuable piece of jewellery and didn't dare to put it on. In fact, he didn't even dare to look at it.

Then the head driver called. The caravan was ready to move on and the merchant had to go. He quickly said goodbye to Mary and Joseph, kissed the baby and hurried away, holding the ring tightly in his clenched hand. Turning round he called: "I'll come back. I promise to help you on your journey home to your own country again, when the time comes."

"The Lord be with you," Mary called back.

***

Joseph and Mary lived in the Egyptian village for many years. Everybody there thought that they were ordinary people. The women often came to their house to have a chat with Mary.

They admired her boy and often praised him. He was so gentle and strong and kind.

"I've never seen a boy like him before in all the land of the Jews," one woman would sometimes say. "He's like an angel from heaven. But Mary, could you lend me a little flour, mine's all finished and my little girl is hungry, she's not nearly as strong and healthy as your boy."

Then Mary would take out her small store of flour, and give it to her neighbour.

"Your child looks like a king's son," another would say. "Something great will happen to him, Mary. But could you lend me some oil, because my jar is completely empty."

And Mary would take out her jar of oil and give it to her neighbour, who would go back to her own home happily with it.

And still, nobody in the village really knew who the child was. But the animals had found out within a few hours of their arrival. First of all it was the dog. He had been sniffing around in the garden and heard the baby gurgling. Mary had put him down in the warm sand under a rustling palm tree. The dog was curious and came close. As soon as he saw that the child had been left on his own, he came up and touched him with his nose.

"Don't hurt him," called the donkey, who was tethered to a tree.

The baby stretched out his little chubby hand and stuck it right into the dog's mouth. The donkey hardly dared to breathe.

"Be careful," he whispered to the child. "Be careful."

But the dog licked the baby's hand very carefully and then began to roll around on the ground and play until the little one was laughing happily.

"Who is this baby?" the dog asked the surprised donkey. "There's something special about him. He's not like other children. It's so lovely to be near him, I have never felt anything like it before. Is he an angel?"

"He is the one who will be the Good Shepherd," the donkey told him.

"What?" cried the dog. "And I licked his face!"

Just then, the neighbour's cat came along waving her tail, ready to jump up on to the roof. It was such fun sitting up there and driving all the dogs mad.

"Come here, cat," shouted the dog eagerly, "come and listen."

The cat was so surprised that she stood still.

"What are you up to now?" she hissed. "Do you think you can trick me?"

"No," said the dog, "but come and see the new baby. Who do you think he is? Guess!"

The baby stretched out his arms to the cat, who shot forward and began to purr and put her front paws gently on him.

"Be careful," warned the dog, "Can't you see who he is?"

"He looks just like an ordinary child," thought the cat, "but it does feel nice when he touches me – the way I was licked when I was little."

"Who is he then?" she asked aloud.

"The Good Shepherd," said the dog.

"The one that the whole world's been waiting for, from the beginning?" asked the cat.

"Yes," said the donkey, "that's him."

Some birds came swooping over the cat's head. They had caught sight of her and thought it'd be fun to tease her.

"Stop that!" called the cat to the birds. "Don't disturb the baby. Can't you see he's just gone to sleep?"

"Who's the baby?" the curious birds wanted to know as they swooped down past the cat again.

"Hey, be careful," said the cat, "you'll wake him."

The birds perched in the tree and looked at the child.

"Come and have a good look at him," said the cat.

"Oh, we should trust you should we?" mocked the birds. "We know what you're like!"

"I won't touch you. I promise," said the cat.

One or two birds risked coming down to the ground, but well out of reach of the cat.

"What a lovely baby! Look how he smiles in his sleep," they chirped.

"Do you know who this baby is?" asked the dog.

"No," said one of the birds, "but he looks like an angel."

"Do you know what angels look like?" asked the cat.

"Yes I do! I was in the Land of Judah in winter and it was full of angels. They were singing because of a child who had come from heaven to a town called Bethlehem."

"I saw them too," said a second bird.

"We were talking to some birds who had come with his mother," chattered a third.

"You should have heard how the angels sang," chirped another. "We could never learn to sing like that, but we did learn a cradle song from those birds and it went like this."

The birds were now all singing so happily, and at the same time so peacefully, that Mary came out and said: "Surely those can't be my birds from Nazareth, can they?"

Smiling, she scattered a handful of corn for them. When they came to eat it she saw that they were not her birds after all.

"That's funny," she said, "you sing just like my little songsters at home."

"But that *is* the child's mother," chirped the birds, "and so that *is* the child the angels sang for."

"That's right," said the dog, "and he will be the Good Shepherd."

"But how did they get here," asked the birds, "right to the banks of the Nile?"

"I'll tell you," said the donkey.

But the little donkey had only just begun when one of the birds cried:

"It *was you* who were with them. You're their little donkey!"

"Yes, yes," piped the other birds, "it's the same little donkey."

And then they listened ever so quietly to everything that the donkey told them about the family's escape into Egypt. When he had finished, the birds said: "We're so glad the Good Shepherd has come here to our country."

"But we're not going to stay here forever," said the donkey.

"Then why did you come here?" the birds wanted to know.

The donkey told them about the wicked king.

"We must work together to make sure that no harm comes to the child," said the cat earnestly. "You birds must be our scouts. As soon as you hear of anything that is not good, come here and tell us. The dog and I will take turns to keep watch when the donkey is away at work. Because Egypt is also a dangerous country, and you never know..."

"Yes, that sounds good," said the dog and the birds. They didn't want anything bad to happen to the baby.

"Is that really necessary?" asked the donkey. "It's so peaceful here."

"Don't you be too sure!" said the dog.

"The angels will help us," said the donkey.

***

In fact, the days went by easily without any disturbance or excitement, other than when a caravan arrived. Then there would be hustle and bustle and shouting for an hour or two, and then the village would settle down, sleepy and quiet again.

And then one day, danger arrived.

King Herod was angry because he hadn't managed to find the baby. So he sent a message to Egypt asking the Egyptians to let his soldiers cross the border to look for the child.

And that is how the soldiers came to the village.

Mary was in the middle of clearing out an old tumbledown hut which stood among some rotting tree trunks. It hadn't been used for many years, and Mary wanted to clear away the rubbish and sweep the cottage clean so that Joseph could keep his tools there. The boy had grown much bigger now and could crawl about. He was playing with the cat outside, while Joseph and the donkey worked in an far corner of the huge gardens.

The soldiers rode up to the village. They went into all the houses asking about the family who had escaped from the Land of Judah. But no one would tell them anything about Joseph and Mary. They searched every house in the village, but couldn't find a trace of them.

The swallows nesting above the door of the first house saw the soldiers, but they didn't know that that meant danger.

Then a shining angel appeared, pointed to Mary's garden and whispered to the swallows: "Quickly, hide the baby!"

The birds flew off at once and chirped together: "Look out! Soldiers! They're looking for the child!"

"Where shall we hide him?" wailed the cat, suddenly frightened.

"Into the hut!" said the dog, rushing up.

The birds flew down to the ground and chirped noisily in front of the boy. He understood straight away what they meant, because he crawled quickly into the dark hut. Mary saw him come in.

"What are you doing in here?" she smiled. She picked him up to take him outside. The birds all fluttered round her head and chirped so urgently that she understood that something unusual was happening. She went out and listened. Then she heard the clip-clop of hooves. Horses! That meant soldiers.

Mary held the baby tightly and shrank back into the hut. Oh, why had she chosen today to sweep it out? Now it looked so clean, the soldiers would certainly look inside. She wanted to run out and find another hiding place.

But the birds fluttered and chirped and sent Mary back inside again. Then some swallows came with spiders in their beaks. They put them on the old trees by the hut and immediately the spiders began to spin a huge web which hung down in front of the doorway. The dog pawed some dust on to the swept floor so that it soon looked as dirty as before. And when the soldiers came to the garden, the cat was lying in front of the doorway of the hut, yawning.

The soldiers looked into the main cottage, but there was no one at home. They took no notice of Joseph and the donkey. They glanced at the little hut, but one of them said: "No one has set foot inside there for years."

"We'd better have a look all the same," said another.

"Go on then," said the first, "if you want a spider's web round your helmet!"

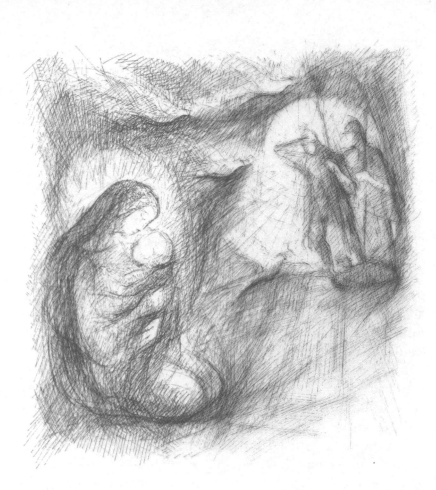

They all laughed and rode away, and soon the thunder of their hooves let everyone know that they were leaving the village.

"Joseph!" called Mary.

Joseph came quickly.

"Soldiers!" said Mary. "They were looking for us."

"Oh!" said Joseph, alarmed. "Praise heaven that they didn't find us!"

"The birds got the boy into the hut and made me stay quiet in there. The dog kicked up earth all over the floor and the spiders filled the doorway with cobwebs almost before I could blink!"

"Ah," said Joseph, "We should never be afraid, because the good angels protect us and they get the animals to help them."

"But Joseph, how do the animals know who the baby is?"

Joseph only shook his head and smiled at Mary, who was already scattering corn for the birds and putting milk into a bowl for the cat and the dog.

The little donkey smiled to himself.

"Thank you, everyone," he said later to the dog and the cat and the birds. "You did very well."

"Yes," said the cat, "didn't we say that we would watch out for the child?"

"And you didn't think it would be necessary, did you?" said the dog, "Well, now you see."

"Hmm," said the little donkey. "But I also said that the angels would help us."

In the meantime, the baby had got his hands full of cobwebs and a big spider was crawling right over his finger. He was sitting quite still, just looking at it.

Good news

From time to time, the rich merchant came to visit. Whenever he passed through the little village he always took time to go out to the balsam garden and visit Joseph and Mary. Sometimes he brought a fine piece of wood for Joseph to make something out of. Sometimes he brought some beautiful material for Mary, and he always brought a present for the boy.

When he came the first time, the boy had just learn to walk.

"He can walk already!" cried the merchant, surprised. "He's very good at it too. Very steady on his feet."

Joseph smiled and said, "All little children learn to walk as long as they've got healthy legs."

The next time the merchant came to visit, the child could talk and say "Father" and "Mother" and a few other simple words.

What a clever child! The merchant had never heard such a young child speak so clearly. Maybe he would be a great speaker in Israel one day.

But Mary laughed and said that he could speak just the same as other children his age.

And then they didn't see the merchant for a long time. Joseph and Mary sometimes talked about him and wondered if he had given up travelling to Egypt. They also wondered whether it would soon be time for them to go home.

No one wanted to travel home more than the donkey. It was nice playing with the boy, who was growing up so fast and learning to walk and talk. But it would be better to be able to share that joy with all his friends back in Nazareth. The little frisky kids and lambs would be all grown up now, but the donkey was sure that they were still longing just as much for Mary and the child. And he could never forget that he had promised to bring them home again. "Sometimes I think I'm beginning to grow old," he thought. "My legs are getting a bit stiff and it's going to be hard for me to cross the desert again. I hope it won't be too long now. My eyes are dimmer than they used to be. What if I couldn't see the angel? What would we do then?"

"Mary," said Joseph one day, "I think our little donkey's beginning to get old. He can't do as much as he used to, and I wonder how his eyes are doing."

Mary lifted up the donkey's head and looked into his eyes.

"They are just as beautiful as before," she said, "and he looks at me so caringly that my heart overflows with love."

"But he stumbled over a tree trunk today, and yesterday he bumped into a tree. He can't properly see where he's going any more."

"My dear," said Mary, "then we must be doubly careful with him."

Joseph and Mary stroked the donkey more often than before, and fed him the best things they could scrape together, and Joseph often carried the load himself, even if he had to go back and forth several times.

That meant that the donkey had plenty of time to play with the child. Joseph had made a saddle and the boy soon learned to ride, even though he was so little. At those times, the donkey's legs didn't feel stiff, and his eyes weren't dim. He galloped off while the little boy cheered and sat up high in the saddle, and all the children of the village came running to watch them. Everyone had a turn at riding.

In between times, the donkey would lie down and rest and the boy would sit beside him and talk and talk.

"They understand each other well," observed Mary.

***

One fine morning Joseph said, "Mary, good news! We're going home!"

"Are we really? Wonderful! How do you know?"

"The angel spoke to me in a dream and said, 'The wicked king has died. Take Mary and the boy with you, and go home to your own country.'"

Mary clapped her hands and her face shone. "Thank you God! Home at last!"

And she lifted the boy up and said: "My child, at last you'll see your home."

"Home?" wondered the boy.

But Joseph looked carefully at the little donkey. Would the donkey be up to it?

That same evening, the quiet village was roused by a merry jingling sound.

"There's a caravan coming," said Mary. "I can hear the camels' bells. I wonder if it's our good friend the merchant."

"Yes, he did promise to help us on our way home. I'm sure God has sent him at this very moment," said Joseph.

And sure enough, it was the merchant.

He was very pleased to see how big the boy had grown.

"Oh, what a fine child!" he cried. "A royal child! And now you can go home, because wicked King Herod is dead. Be ready early tomorrow morning, and we'll start our journey though the desert."

The journey home

"Well, well!" said the camels, "if it isn't Mary's little donkey! Are you going home now? That's nice!"

Two new camels introduced themselves with their very best manners, then said, "Are you Mary's little donkey? We've been told you're the cleverest donkey in the world, and that you can see angels. Is that true?"

"I used to be able to," said the donkey, "but I must confess my eyes have grown a bit dim lately, so I'm not sure if I can now."

"I'm sure you'll be able to, if necessary," said the oldest camel kindly.

So the long journey home began. The boy gave a happy shout when he was allowed to ride a camel, but as soon as the company stopped for a rest, he ran to the little donkey, holding him by the neck and whispering secrets into the donkey's ear.

"I'm no good any more," thought the donkey sadly. "I'm only a burden."

The little boy seemed to understand, because he told the donkey that he was his best friend in the whole world, and that he needed the donkey very much. The donkey felt less tired, and his feet stopped aching. He rubbed his nose against the boy's cheek.

"He has healing in his hands," the donkey told the camels.

They thought so too, because when one of them got a bad bite from a horse-fly, he got better again when the boy laid his cool hand on the burning swelling.

This time the journey went well. No sandstorm came sweeping along to force the travellers to seek shelter, and when they came to the wells, they found them full of water.

But the nights were not so peaceful. Lots of wild animals

roamed around the caravan when it was time to set up camp, and as soon as night fell, the travellers sensed a fearsome prowling going on around them in the darkness. Jackals howled so eerily that the blood froze in the men's veins, and the roar of the lions rolled like thunder over the desert. The travellers kept their fires burning all night, and the camel drivers took turns at keeping watch.

One night it was worse than ever. There was more roaring and howling and barking than anyone had ever heard before, and only the little boy could sleep through it. The camels and the donkey trembled. The men were anxious and uneasy. At last everyone fell asleep and towards morning, even the watchmen dozed off.

The moon stood high in the sky, shining so brightly that it was almost like daytime. The desert sands gleamed like silver. The little donkey woke up because it was suddenly so silent all around.

He stood for a moment blinking in the soft moonlight, and his dim eyes looked out over the desert. He thought about how beautiful it was.

"That's good," he thought. "The wild animals have gone away. They've realised at last that it's no use coming too near, because the fire is burning all night. It's good to have a fire, it protects us and scares them away. Well, I think I can sleep for a bit longer. It's not morning yet. Mary is sleeping soundly, and Joseph, and the little..."

The donkey blinked, then he looked again, but no, he couldn't see the boy. He got very worried and he started to walk around the camp, searching. Not a trace of the child anywhere.

"Where is he?" panicked the donkey. "Where? A lion couldn't have... no impossible! But where is he?... Perhaps a lion..."

The donkey searched through the camp once more. No sign of the boy. The poor donkey wandered out alone into the desert. He had to find out what had happened to the child.

"Have wild animals killed him? If they have, they might as well kill me too. What is there left to live for?" he thought miserably.

A little way away, some big bright stones stood out sharply against the sky. The donkey went towards them, but when he got nearer he smelled the smell of lions. He stopped suddenly because it seemed a bit grizzly just to walk straight into the wild beasts' mouths. His whole body was trembling. And then, he heard a happy little laugh. The boy!

The donkey went forward carefully and called to his little friend. Soon he saw that the stones were alive. They were huge lions, lying in a circle around the child who was sitting on the ground. One of the lions knocked him over playfully but carefully with his mighty paw. The boy rolled over. He certainly thought it was a good game because he was soon on his feet shouting "again," and once more the lion pushed him over. Then he went up to the lion and playfully blew into his eyes. The donkey hardly dared to breathe, but the lion didn't mind. Then the boy tickled the lion's big nose and the lion curled up and purred like a giant cat.

Another lion nudged the boy gently in the ribs, asking to be stroked, while the jackals lay around wagging their tails. One of them pushed his way in among the lions and licked the boy's foot.

Then the boy noticed the little donkey and called out happily. The lions turned round and looked at the donkey, who felt himself trembling worse than before.

"Don't be afraid," said one of the lions. "We won't hurt you tonight. But why won't the humans let us meet the Good Shepherd?"

"How did you know it was him?" asked the donkey, astonished.

"The birds in Egypt have spread the news far and wide, and we have followed him all this time to see him and meet him, but the humans wouldn't let us."

"They didn't understand that's what you wanted," said the donkey.

"But tonight he came out himself to meet us. We all gave one hugh shout altogether, and he woke up and came out to us and he wasn't afraid, not a bit."

"Oh no, he's not afraid of anything," said the donkey. "But why do you want to meet him? Wild animals don't need a shepherd, do they?"

"Don't you know," answered the lion, "that it has been said: 'The day shall come when all animals shall be friends and live in peace with one another. Panthers and lions shall live together with cows and donkeys and lambs, and a little child shall lead them.' And who else could that child be, if not this one? The Good Shepherd!" And the huge animal laid his head humbly against the child's leg.

"But how do you know all this?" asked the donkey in wonder.

"God has made it true it from the beginning of time. The wind speaks about it and the water sings about it. You just need to take the time to listen. Isn't that true, little one?"

The boy nodded earnestly.

"We knew straight away it was him," said another lion, "because when he came we felt so safe and peaceful, and no one could harm anyone else."

Now a third lion arrived.

"Would you like a ride?" he asked, and lay down. The boy understood, because he tried to climb up on to the back of the powerful animal. Finally he succeeded and he sat there proudly holding on to the lion's mane. Then the ride began; and you've never seen anything like it! The lion bounded along and the boy shouted with delight.

Meanwhile back in the camp, Joseph had woken up. He immediately woke the other men up and they armed themselves with sticks and burning firebrands, and went in search of the child, fearing the worst.

Suddenly, the boy appeared, riding on the back of the lion! Ten steps away from the astonished men the lion stopped, lay down on the ground and let the child slide off his back. Then the lion turned round and disappeared as quickly as he had come.

Joseph gave the boy a huge hug. "Where have you been?"

"With the wild animals."

"But why? Didn't you know it was dangerous?"

"They called me, and so I went."

"We were all so afraid," said Joseph.

"But it wasn't dangerous at all," said the boy. "The animals were all so nice."

"What kind of child is that?" wondered the camel drivers. "He was riding on a lion as proudly as a king on his horse. Are we dreaming?"

The next night the boy woke up again when the animals called him. Joseph told him to lie down again; but the boy answered that the animals were longing to see him. He just had to go.

"Go then, my dear," said Mary. "You'll be as safe among the animals of the wild as among the dogs and cats of Egypt. No animal can hurt you."

For three nights, the boy played with the animals in the desert. He had the same fun each time, and more and more animals came along. On the last night the lions took him to a little oasis miles away, where little monkeys picked tasty fruit for him.

In the morning no one in the camp believed his story, but when he brought out a bunch of dates they were all amazed. The head driver said: "We used to be amazed that Mary's little donkey could see angels, but this child is even more amazing. Is he an angel that has come down to earth? Who else could be as safe among the wild beasts as he is on his mother's knee?"

***

The days were very, very hot in the desert, and the journey was just a long as before. But the little boy was so radiantly happy and cheerful that everyone forgot about how tired and thirsty they were. They couldn't be unfriendly or in a bad mood when he was about.

"Well, well, look!" said the camels one day. "Have we got through the desert already? Over there are the mountains of Judah."

"This journey has passed so quickly," said the camel drivers. "We'll soon be there."

When they came to the place where the road branched off to Jerusalem, Joseph and Mary had to leave their fellow travellers.

"Many, many thanks for all your help," said Joseph to the merchant.

"I have been very well rewarded," he replied.

"Was the ring that valuable?" asked Joseph, wonderingly.

"The ring! Certainly it is very, very valuable, and I haven't yet dared to put it on. Maybe I'll try it soon. But I meant that it has been a great joy to help you and Mary and the boy, and to be your friend is reward enough."

"You are so good," said Mary. "We'll never forget you. If your travels bring you to Nazareth any time, do come and visit us."

"I have never travelled through that town, but for you I will go there. I must see how the boy is growing up. I tell you, one day he will be great."

"Farewell, little donkey," said the camels. "Perhaps we'll never meet again, but we'll never forget you and Joseph and Mary and the child. No one has ever been as good to us as they have, and when the boy is around the camel drivers are much more friendly than normal. They don't drive us so hard and they give us more to eat."

"Goodbye," said the little donkey. "I'll never forget all your help."

Joseph and Mary stood and watched the caravan moving away as it headed for Jerusalem. They still had a few days' journey to the north, but it was along well-known roads, and they would be meeting people from their own country. They were back in their home. It was early spring and it smelled of thousands of flowers. The donkey snatched at some green blades.

"I'd forgotten how good the grass tastes here at home," he thought.

"My dear little donkey," said Mary, "now you must carry all our baggage home. Will you manage that?"

The donkey twitched his long tail happily.

"Look Joseph, how lively he is! He knows we'll soon be home."

"But it's a big load," said Joseph. "The merchant has given us so many presents."

"I can walk the whole way," said Mary. "I feel so refreshed now that I can breathe the air of our own country again. The boy can walk too, he's so big and strong now. Look how lightly he runs about. And if need be, I can carry him sometimes."

"Yes, that way we'll manage fine," said Joseph. "And I can take some of the baggage on my back."

So they travelled towards Nazareth, Joseph with a big bundle on his back, the little donkey loaded with as much as he could carry and Mary with the little boy. He danced on ahead of them so lightly that it seemed like he had invisible wings.

The long waiting

"We've been away such a long time now," said Joseph, "that I don't think anyone will remember us any more."

"Oh yes, they will," said Mary. "My sister will be thinking of us, you can be sure. And all our friends. And the animals at home."

Yes, there were many who remembered them and missed them.

***

First, there was the old man who owned the tumbledown stable in Bethlehem.

"I wonder what happened to them," he would say when he met the shepherds. "I can't get them out of my thoughts. They escaped from wicked Herod, but how could they survive in the desert? I'm sure his soldiers caught up with them and killed them."

"The desert is also very dangerous for lone travellers," said the shepherds. "We're afraid that bad things happened to them."

"How can you talk like that?" said the youngest shepherd, who was called Reuben. "Could God have let them die when he himself sent the child to earth? No, I believe they are all right, somewhere far away. And now that King Herod's dead they'll come back, you'll see. I'd just love to see the child again. Do you remember that night?"

"Yes; do you remember the shining ring round the child's head?" said Reuben's grandfather, "Almost like a crown, and it was only starlight shining on him."

"I'll never forget the angels' song," said Reuben's father.

"I wish they'd come back soon," sighed the old man in the stable. "I feel like I haven't got much longer to live. My heart tells me that."

"They'll come soon," said Reuben, "and I'm longing to see their little donkey too. I liked him a lot."

***

In a little town not very far from Bethlehem there lived three men who also often talked about Joseph and Mary. They were honest men, but they had once been robbers.

"Wasn't it a wonderful feeling the morning we left the robbers' den," the young one would say. "It was so good to go to work, and not just go and dream up wicked plans."

"Yes, and I really enjoyed the birds singing that first time," the second went on.

"But since then," mused the oldest, "we have often found it hard to earn a living and we've been hungry sometimes."

"More than once I've been tempted to go out and steal," said the youngest.

"I don't think I can stay honest for much longer," said the second. "When I get hungry, I feel my fingers itching."

"It would be marvellous if Mary came here," exclaimed the oldest. "If only I could see her and talk to her, I'd be able to put up with being poor again."

"Me too," said the friend of the birds.

"And me," added the youngest. "But I don't think we'll see her again."

"I wonder what happened to them," said the oldest.

***

There was a poor house where Joseph and Mary and the donkey had stayed on the first night of their journey to Bethlehem. The children still talked about it.

"They're never going to come back!" said the older girl. "And Mary promised that I could hold her little baby."

"And I was going to look after the donkey," said the boy who had cried for a long time because his father hadn't got a donkey. "And I've got so much hay for the donkey now, it'll last a whole year!"

He had been gathering hay all this time and he had a big, big pile.

"Remember how nice it was," said his big sister, "when they let us go some of the way with them."

"And they let us ride the donkey," said the others. "It was the best treat we ever had."

"I really do want to see Mary," sighed the older sister. "No one is as good and gentle as she is."

"I want to play with her baby," said the little one, who had now grown into quite a big girl.

***

But of course the ones who missed them most were those at home in Nazareth.

"Why hasn't Mary come home?" sighed her sister. "I wonder where she is."

"They'll never come home again," said her husband. The sister was very upset.

"I can't look after her animals much longer," she complained. "It takes too much time to care for them and get food as well, especially when I've got my own animals too. It was all right as long as old Judith was able to help, but now she can't walk at all and I have to lend her a hand instead."

"We'll have to sell the animals," said her husband, "and we'd better sell the house and the bit of land too."

"No, no!" cried the wife, "we can't do that. At least not yet! What if they came back?"

"The rich potter said yesterday that he would like to buy the lot. He'll give us a good price."

"Not yet. Wait a bit," his wife begged. "I'll manage a bit longer."

"The potter wants to buy right away," said the man.

"But he's not a nice man," sighed the sister. "Mary's animals will have a rough time with him, and they're not used to anything but kindness. No, let me try for a bit longer."

***

But it was Mary's animals who missed them most of all.

"Where's the little donkey?" the little lambs and kids had wailed while they were growing up. They were no longer lambs

126

and kids, of course, but fully grown sheep and goats, but they still missed them just as much. They told their own lambs and kids how Mary would be coming home soon, and that she would have her little child with her. And she would be riding on the best, cleverest donkey in the whole world.

"Are they coming soon, mother?" bleated the new little lambs.

And the new little kids sprang about and kept on asking: "Do you think they'll come tomorrow, mother?"

"Don't pester so much," said the old nanny goat, "or they won't come at all."

The birds of Nazareth felt the same. They had flown home with the news of the birth of the child and there had been a great celebration among the animals of Nazareth. They had all believed that Joseph and Mary would come home with their child in just a few days. But Mary and Joseph had been gone a long time. What had happened to them?

The birds waited and waited, but they didn't forget. Again and again new little birds sat in their nests and chirped: "Are they coming soon, mother?"

Happy travellers

Although hardly anyone knew it, Joseph and Mary were finally on their way home, with the donkey and the little boy.

As they approached Bethlehem Mary said, "We must go and visit the old man. He was so good to us."

The donkey trotted lightly along the road he knew so well. No angel was needed to show him which way to go.

The old man was so happy to see them! He talked and talked.

"You've come back at last!" he said. "I should have known that something was going to happen, because last night I dreamed I was walking in the gardens of paradise, and that could only mean that God intends to take me there soon. My heart can't cope with earthly life any more. But I didn't want to die before I had seen you and the child again. He's grown up so big and strong. He looks just like the angels I saw in my dream last night. And tomorrow you must say hello to the shepherds when you go by."

"Oh!" said Mary surprised. "Haven't they forgotten us?"

"Forgotten you!" said the old man. "Who could ever forget you!"

And so they slept in the stable again that night. Of course, the boy was much too big for the crib. He lay on the straw between the black cow and the sheep.

"Fancy seeing him again," they whispered contentedly to each other.

***

Reuben had taken his sheep to the pasture land to graze. He was almost fully grown now, a powerful lad with broad shoulders and an open, honest face.

"Reuben's a good shepherd," his grandfather had said that

morning, "and he can pasture the sheep by himself now it's such good weather."

And so the other shepherds were sitting at home, resting.

Reuben stood high up at the top of a hill looking out over the country.

"Oh, I wish I could see him again!" he cried to the scurrying clouds. "The Prince of Peace of the House of David. The Good Shepherd, who will be a shepherd to all people. Can't you who fly so high above the earth tell me where he is?"

The clouds didn't answer. But when Reuben was a little boy, he had been given a two-week-old lamb. Of course the lamb was now an old sheep, but she was still his favourite animal. The old sheep now butted him in the back of his knees and brushed against him, saying, "Reuben, he's on his way here. Didn't you hear the birds chirping about it at dawn this morning? They said he was in Bethlehem in the old stable."

But Reuben didn't understand what the sheep was saying. He only thought she was bleating in a rather strange way.

"Yes, yes," he said, stroking her. "I see you want to comfort me, but how can you do that?"

"If only you understood what I'm saying, you *would* be comforted," thought the sheep.

But Reuben sighed. Then he caught sight of some travellers coming along a little path.

"Who are they?" he thought, "A donkey with a big load, a man and a woman. And a boy running in front of them – no, it can't be...!"

He shouted with happiness. "It's Mary's little donkey! No other donkey in the whole world holds his head up like that. And he's trotting along as neatly as ever, although it looks as if he's getting old and a bit stiff in the legs."

Reuben rushed down the hill and ran to meet them. And sure enough, it was Joseph and Mary. But could that boy, who looked so bright and lively, be the same gentle baby from the crib?

Reuben stopped. The boy smiled and held out his hand. A beautiful butterfly had settled on his finger.

"Look," he said cheerfully.

Then Reuben recognised the shine in his eyes. It *was* Mary's child, the little baby for whom the angels had sung. And Reuben jumped high into the air with gladness and shouted with joy.

All the sheep gathered round the donkey to hear how he had led Joseph and Mary to safety in Egypt.

"You are such a clever donkey," they said, "the best in the whole world."

"I didn't manage it all by myself," said the donkey. "At first I was helped by the good angel, and then also by the big camels."

"We've always heard that camels are proud beasts," said the sheep.

"Oh no, they're very kind and clever."

Reuben brought the travellers home with him to the other shepherds. Then there was a great celebration. They made a great feast and many shepherds from other areas came to see the child they'd heard so much about. The old shepherds told them the story again and again of the night they had heard the angels' song, and how they'd gone to Bethlehem and found the baby in the manger.

But the little boy didn't want to just sit still and be admired. He helped Reuben look after the donkey and to shut the sheep in their pens for the night.

He was strong now, and he had never been afraid. When the big billy goat came and shook his huge horns right in front of him, he just laughed and patted the billy goat's nose. The goat felt a bit silly and became friendly.

And the boy enjoyed watching Reuben look after the sheep, and hearing him talk about how to find the best wells and the greenest grass.

"I'm going to be a shepherd when I grow up," the child explained. "A good shepherd who is always on the look out in case his sheep start wandering off."

"You will be the Good Shepherd of all people," said Reuben. "And I will follow you wherever you go."

The little one took Reuben by the hand.

"Do you really mean that?" he asked eagerly.

"Yes, I really do mean it," said Reuben. "I decided on that when I saw you in the manger."

"Oh, that's wonderful!" said the boy. "You and I can be shepherd's together!"

***

Up on a cliff, three men stood looking out.

"There are some travellers over there," said the eldest. "Shall we rob them?"

"No," said the two others.

"But we could get some money to buy better tools," he said persuasively. "We'd find it easier to get work."

"If we start robbing again now, we'll never be able to stop again," objected one of the others. "We'd better not try."

"Oh, if only I could talk to Mary," sighed the second one to himself. "I could cope with the hunger and thirst a little better."

"Look," said the older man, "it's only two people and their donkey, and he has a mighty big load."

"You can't tell what's in it at this distance," objected the youngest.

"We can go half way towards them anyway," said the eldest. "We can hide behind those rocks and easily attack them when they come out of the ravine. But if they seem to be poor, we just stay where we are and let them go on. They won't see us."

The others weren't very happy, but they went along to wait behind the big rocks. The eldest said: "I'll take on the first one that comes if he looks as if he has anything worth taking, and then you take on the second. Don't need to hit them so hard that they'd be badly hurt. Then we'll take the donkey and his load and be off."

So there all three of them stood there, waiting.

"That's odd," thought the first, "it smells like fresh spring flowers, like in our hut that night when Joseph and Mary were there. Can the scent really come all the way here from the fields of Bethlehem?"

"Strange," thought the second. "What a lot of birds there

are! I haven't heard the birds singing like this since the birds of Nazareth sang for us."

But the third one had already heard footsteps. He gripped his heavy stick and got ready to attack – when a little boy shot forward out of the narrow gap in the rocks.

The man was so surprised that he stood still with his stick raised. The child turned and saw him. He called a cheerful "hello" and held out a loaf of bread which he was carrying.

The man dropped his stick, but before he could decide whether to take the loaf, the child had put it in his hand. Then the child ran back and said something to his parents.

"Good gracious Joseph", cried the woman, "it's the good men from the hut in the mountains!" She stepped forward and held out her hand to the three men.

"I'm so happy to see you again," she smiled. "I've often thought of you."

"Mary," all three of them cried together, "is it really you?"

Then they were all talking at once, Joseph and Mary and the three men. The boy had got hold of the robber's stick and was using it as a play horse.

"How are you getting on?" asked Joseph.

"Badly sometimes, not much better at other times," said the eldest. "We've not had much luck getting work for a long time now."

"It's been a long time since we had enough to eat," said the youngest.

"You must eat with us today," said Mary firmly. "Look, sit down here and we'll rest for a bit."

Joseph brought out food from the baggage.

"Hmm, work," he said. "In Bethlehem I met a man who needed men in his vineyard. Go there and you'll get..."

"No one will hire us," interrupted the youngest gloomily, "because our tools aren't good enough."

Mary looked at Joseph, who nodded and took out his purse.

"Here you are," he said and offered the young man a gold coin. "That will do for tools for all three of you."

"But we can't take your money," protested the eldest. "You need it yourselves."

"I got it from a good merchant, and a present brings more happiness when it is passed on," said Joseph, laying the coin in the man's hand.

"I knew that everything would be better and easier as soon as you came back!" exclaimed the man. "And how amazing that you came today! To be honest, we'd almost turned to robbery again."

"The ways of God are wonderful," said Joseph.

"And this is your boy," said the youngest. "He's so big already! What's his name?"

"My name is Jesus," said the boy easily. "It means 'helper'."

"Quite right," the man smiled "and who are you going to help?"

"Everyone!" said the boy.

"I believe you will," said the man, "if you grow to be like your parents. I've never met anyone who has helped me as much as they have done."

***

A few days later the travellers reached the little village where they had stopped the first night.

"We'll soon be home," said Mary. "Won't that be wonderful. Think how many years have gone by. And you, my child, you've never seen your home! But soon you'll be able to open its doors, and meet all the animals."

"All the sheep and the goats and the lambs and the kids," asked the boy, "are they my animals too, mother?"

"Yes, they're yours too, We'll look after them together, you and me."

"Can I take them out to graze? And give them food and water?"

"You can come with me every day and do that," promised Mary. "But you'll also help your father, and learn to plane wood, and saw, and use a chisel."

The boy began to dance along the road in front of the donkey. And the worn-out animal thought about the lovely meadows in Nazareth and of his friends waiting at home there, and he neighed happily.

"There's a village behind the hills," said Joseph. "We'll look for somewhere to sleep because we won't reach home tonight."

Suddenly the donkey started to move quickly because he badly wanted to get there and rest.

Joseph picked the little boy up and carried him in his arms while the sun set. The child fell asleep at once with his head on his father's shoulder.

When they came to the village street, Joseph stood hesitating, but the donkey trotted on.

"See," said Mary, "the donkey knows where to go. It's a long time since he's done that. Perhaps he's seen the angel again."

The donkey had recognised a voice, a very good friend's voice. He had heard the bright little boy who had once promised to gather hay for him. The donkey had heard him shouting in the distance. Now the boy saw the donkey. He rushed towards him and threw himself on his neck.

"They're here, they're here!" he called.

Then Mary recognised the boy and his sisters.

"O Joseph, how clever our little donkey is. He remembered that we promised to visit these people on our way home, and we'd forgotten. Lucky he saved us from breaking our promise."

So they went with the boy to his home. The big sister was allowed to carry the sleeping child, but the lively boy led the donkey into the stable and helped Joseph to unload the bags. Then he opened the trap door of a little hay loft, and showed Joseph all the good hay. Joseph was amazed. He had never dreamed that the boy would keep his promise as well as this.

There was lots of celebrating in the house as the unexpected guests came inside. They were poor and didn't have much to offer, but Mary brought out honey cake and other tasty food the merchant had given her. The children had never seen such a feast.

"The richest farmer in the village held a feast yesterday, and we weren't invited," said a little one, "but now we've got a much better feast than anyone else."

Yes, her brother and sisters thought so too.

The big sister undressed Mary's sleeping child, washed him and put him in bed, while the others watched. "Isn't he lovely!" she said.

"Oh yes," said all the little ones, "What's his name?"

"His name is Jesus," replied Joseph.

***

The next morning, the children were allowed to accompany the travellers for some of the way, just as they had done years before.

"What shall we do with all the hay?" enquired the bright lad. "The donkey has only eaten a little bit. Can you take it in sacks for him?"

No, Joseph couldn't do that, and anyway the donkey was too heavily laden already.

"But what shall I do with all the hay? We don't have a donkey." said the boy, sadly. "I've told father many times he ought to buy one but he doesn't seem to want to."

"No, because he can't afford it," said his big sister. "You shouldn't go on pestering him."

"But it would be so nice to have a donkey," said the boy. "He and I could work in the vineyard and earn some money! But no one will lend us money for a donkey, even though I would pay it back later."

"I'm sure you would," said Joseph, "and so I'll lend you a gold piece."

The boy couldn't believe his ears.

"Are you rich?" he asked, "We all thought you were poor."

"We *are* poor," said Mary, "but poor people must help each other. Joseph got some money from a rich merchant, and it's good to pass the gifts on."

It is impossible to describe how happy the children were! They laughed and shouted with joy, and jumped about, but happiest of all was Mary's little boy. He clapped his hands when the boy with the gold piece in his hand turned somersaults on the ground in front of Joseph.

***

By the afternoon it was still a long way to Nazareth. It had been a hard day, and Joseph thought that they should stay with someone they knew in a neighbouring village, and do the last bit of the journey the next day. He was tired, Mary was tired and the donkey was hardly able to take a step. The only one who didn't show any signs of tiredness was Jesus, who ran cheerfully beside the donkey, chatting away.

Even so, the exhausted animal refused to stop. He just went on and on, although Joseph shouted that they should rest.

"Joseph, what's wrong with the little donkey?" asked Mary surprised.

"He can't be seeing the angel now," said Joseph. "There's no danger here. And we know the way exactly. Stop here, little friend."

But the donkey didn't stop and the boy kept going as well. The two understood each other so well.

"Do you think the donkey's seen an angel?" Mary asked the little boy.

"I've just seen an angel myself," said the boy. "He beckoned for us to hurry. I told the donkey and he started to hurry."

"Then we'd better just keep on going until we get home," said Joseph.

"Of course," said Mary. "Just keep thinking that we'll soon be home."

"Home it is," said Joseph, hitching his load higher on his back.

In Nazareth

That very afternoon, the rich potter came to Mary's sister and her husband and said:

"I will buy Joseph's house and piece of land today. I must start my new building."

"Not yet," cried Mary's sister. "Wait until autumn."

"By autumn my new pottery must be ready," said the potter. The husband agreed and so they both went out to have a look at the little house belonging to Joseph and Mary.

"The trees will have to go!" said the potter. "I'll send a man to chop them down tomorrow."

"And the animals?"

"Kill the old ones, then sell the young ones to the cattle dealer. He's getting ready to go to market tomorrow. So you'll have to sell them this evening."

And the two of them went off to finish the deal.

There was a lot of alarm among the animals. The sheep bleated in despair, the goats butted with their horns and stamped with their hooves, trying to get through the fence. And all Mary's birds! Were all the trees, where they had their nests, be cut down? What a disaster!

"Is Mary coming home? Is there no sign of the donkey over there in the hills?"

The birds flew off to have a look.

"Any sign of them?" called the sheep.

"Can you see them at all?" cried the goats.

"There *are* some travellers coming. They're still far away," said the birds, "but they've got a donkey."

"It must be them," said the sheep.

"Who else could it be?" said the goats.

The birds flew off to meet them. And sure enough it *was* Joseph and Mary and the donkey! But who was the lively little boy leading the donkey? And *where* was the little baby that Mary had given birth to in Bethlehem? The birds were very disappointed.

"Oh how stupid you are!" said a clever dove. "Don't you realise that the baby has grown so big because they've been away for so long?"

"Yes of course!" And they sung a song of joy that rose to heaven, and called all the other birds of Nazareth to join in.

Joseph lifted the boy onto the donkey's back.

"You shall ride into Nazareth," he said.

The boy gave a shout, the donkey held his head high and trotted along as lightly as when he was young. Mary and Joseph laughed and the birds trilled and chirped and sang with all their might.

And so, they entered Nazareth.

"What's going on?" wondered the people and they ran out to see. "Who's that coming in the light of the setting sun? See how it's shining around them. Have they come from paradise? And that singing of the birds, what does it mean? Or is it angels who are singing?"

"No, it can't be angels," said others. "It's only a boy laughing and shouting. But who are they?" And then they saw that it was Joseph and Mary. The neighbours went out to meet them.

Mary's sister came out into the street. She was crying because her husband was about to sell Mary and Joseph's house.

Then the neighbours called out: "Cheer up! Your sister's here!"

She was so happy, and her husband was too! He thanked God that Mary and Joseph had come back while their house was still there. The potter was annoyed at first, of course, but he soon got over it and said he was glad that they hadn't done the wrong thing.

"Come in, come in," invited Mary's sister, and she lifted the boy off the donkey. "Come in and have something to eat."

"First we have to go home," said Mary. "We've been longing for it every day for many years, and the boy needs to see his house at last."

"But you'll come back won't you?" said her sister. "I want to see more of your little boy. What's his name?"

"My name is Jesus," said the boy. "You can come home with us."

So Mary's sister put him back on the donkey and went with them to Joseph and Mary's cottage.

***

The animals were absolutely quiet when everyone arrived. The birds had already told them the good news and now they all stood, packed tightly together, trembling with hope.

"Here I am!" said the little donkey. "It's been a long journey. But look who I've got on my back!"

They all saw him for the first time. Joseph lifted the boy off and Mary opened the gate and went in to the animals, who pressed round her. They all nudged and gently pushed to be stroked.

"My dear, dear animals," said Mary, "did you miss us very much? I've thought about you so much."

The boy held out his arms to all of them. "Come here, all my little lambs," he whispered happily.

And the lambs and the kids came nearer cautiously and sniffed his hands and let themselves be patted.

"He's got such lovely, friendly hands," they whispered to each other.

"Am I a shepherd now, mother," he asked, "now that I've got sheep and goats?"

"Yes, now you're a shepherd," smiled Mary.

"The Good Shepherd," whispered the sheep and goats. "Our Shepherd."

And the birds of Nazareth sang:

"The Good Shepherd has come home.
He's come home at last,
And God is good."

"Oh, how good and clever you are, little donkey," said all the animals, when the donkey had told them about the long journey. "It was so good that you could see the angel."

"I didn't see him on the way home," said the donkey, "because my eyesight isn't very good anymore. But it didn't matter because the boy saw him, and then we just had to go where the angel wanted us to. But dear me, I *am* tired now, and my legs hurt so much you wouldn't believe it."

"Well you can rest now, little donkey," said the animals. "You have truly earned it, and we're so glad you're home. We've missed you so much! But you really are home at last. The child has come home too, and Mary."

"Yes, and Joseph," said the oldest sheep.

"And the cleverest donkey in the whole world," said a little kid, scampering round with joy.

Share the wonderful story of Mary's Little Donkey

*Also available as a picture book
and a traditional advent calendar*

Adapted for younger children from Gunhild Sehlin's classic chapter book, this charming picture book edition is sumptuously illustrated by Hélène Muller, with marvellous details of the Holy Land.

Open each window in the beautiful traditional Advent calendar to unfold the story of Mary and Joseph's journey to Bethlehem with the help of a very special little donkey.

florisbooks.co.uk

Christ Legends

Selma Lagerlöf

The stories of Jesus' birth and childhood are well known, but Selma Lagerlöf brings them truly to life in this wonderful collection of tales for children.

Her storytelling draws vividly on the colourful history and landscape of the Holy Land. She weaves in a cast of lively characters whose experiences and points of view are not usually represented: a war-hardened soldier at Herod's feast, a grumpy shepherd, Emperor Tiberius himself. Together they proclaim the human drama and divine mystery of the events of Christ's life.

florisbooks.co.uk

Stories of the Saints
A Collection for Children

Siegwart Knijpenga

What can children learn from the lives and actions of the saints?

Stories and legends of the saints have been passed down throughout history. The lives of these remarkable people provide richly inspiring material for children to read, or listen to.

This enjoyable and interesting selection of tales and legends includes over forty saints, ranging from well-known heroes like St Francis and Joan of Arc, to less known but equally colourful characters from a wide range of periods and places.

The stories are suitable for children aged between about seven and eleven.

florisbooks.co.uk